Redder Days

www.penguin.co.uk

Also by Sue Rainsford

Follow Me to Ground

Redder Days

Sue Rainsford

doubleday

TRANSWORLD PUBLISHERS
Penguin Random House, One Embassy Gardens,
8 Viaduct Gardens, London SW11 7BW
www.penguin.co.uk

Transworld is part of the Penguin Random House group of companies
whose addresses can be found at global.penguinrandomhouse.com

Penguin
Random House
UK

First published in Great Britain in 2021 by Doubleday
an imprint of Transworld Publishers

A CIP catalogue record for this book
is available from the British Library.

ISBN 9780857526793

Typeset in 11.88/17.55pt Berling LT Std by Jouve (UK), Milton Keynes
Printed and bound in Great Britain by Clays Ltd, Elcograf S.p.A.

The authorized representative in the EEA is Penguin Random House Ireland,
Morrison Chambers, 32 Nassau Street, Dublin D02 YH68.

Penguin Random House is committed to a sustainable
future for our business, our readers and our planet. This book
is made from Forest Stewardship Council® certified paper.

MIX
Paper from
responsible sources
FSC
www.fsc.org   FSC® C018179

1

For Conor – my heart

'My art is grounded in the belief of one
universal energy which runs through
everything . . . the ancestral sap, the original
beliefs, the primordial accumulations, the
unconscious thoughts that animate the world.'
Ana Mendieta

'Dazzlement is night at noon, the darkness
that reigns at the heart of all that is excessive.'
Michel Foucault, *History of Madness*

'Red is red is red is red.'
Alice Lyons, *Oona*

Koan
Vol. 109
#35

To begin with, we established the timeline. Or rather, the timeline made itself known. Following this, we assumed that – no matter what else came to pass – this allotment of days would remain the most vital, most pressing element of what lay before us. And so: that was what we focused on. Time. Months, weeks, days. What was achievable inside them.

Then, there were certain changes. Changes in strata, substrata. Scarlet alterations across vegetal and animal. We understood that these changes would have to be tracked and traced as precisely as possible and for as long as possible. Everything. All of it. Tweaks in growth, tweaks in shape. Deviations of pelt and spoor.

There was no way for us to know that these initial changes were only the first meagre hint of what was coming.

We'd yet to see, after all, how it unfurled inside our own species.

How it impacted the two-legged and carnal.

A glimmer of puce in a woman's eyes, a child's back with its fuzz of copper fur. Biological ripples that spoke to an interior horror, to a particular kind of damage – that signalled we were now vessels for a very particular kind of rupture.

We knew it was entwined, somehow, with the abbreviated timeframe – perhaps, a kind of cleansing. The planet, thus distressed, had found a new way to purge. But we did not know why every body it moved through it moved through like a storm. Why it turned a person to rough hands and probing tongues, why it landed in the body as an unrelenting fever. But this is the cruelty of any storm; irrespective of its size and point of origin, it is without motivation or vendetta. No storm is subject to reason. If you are destroyed by a storm, it is simply because of where you were standing at the time.

In short, there was nothing to do but accept it.

Let our fears and beliefs settle around it.

> *Red wind, red sun, red hurricane.*
> *That's when we start running.*
> *But block your ears and stuff your mouth,*
>   *when you see the red man coming.*

part i

Stain

Tabatha

I should know by now. What I'll say and how I'll say it.

Maybe, to start, they can decide what they want to ask me straight out and what'll keep for another day.

But no matter what they want to know last or first – I'd hoped my own thoughts would've settled enough that I'd be able to explain the bones of it.

Not all of it. Probably never all of it. But parts of it.

The beginning parts from before they were born. Those months at the very start when, as soon as you woke up in the morning, you were panicking. A bird has just flown into a window, a curtain has just caught fire. That feeling but times a thousand and it hurt, the constant alert – the body taut where it had once been soft, callused where it had once been smooth. A barbed-wire feeling wound through every waking moment and you would do anything to lessen it; to have back your old way of breathing, your old way of sitting still.

The middle parts, the parts they grew up inside of. Their childhood, adolescence. The time we lived together. What made them different from us: they were born into knowledge we had to learn slow, born knowing that surviving meant making your own body strange to you. Making the best pieces of yourself numb. Those pieces that made you a person and not a tree or a house cat – those, you cut out.

And then, the last parts. Tapering parts. Severing parts.

When it was all you could do not to scream. When scream-ing was all your body wanted to do: middle of the night, start of the day. When you couldn't remember a time your jaw wasn't panging from keeping the scream down in your gut. It had come back, the clench up and down your whole body. The barbed wire had come back and we had to get away.

How will that sound, out loud? *We had to get away.*

From rituals we shouldn't have practised, from sacri-fices we shouldn't have made.

That was the last thing that tied us together, when the rest of it was gone. We'd all done things we should not have done. No matter the type of person you were; someone as cautious as me, someone as sharp as their mother. We'd each done at least one thing we wished we had not done. At least one thing for which we'd never be forgiven. No matter if you lived a hundred years and asked for it with blood in your mouth every day – forgiveness wasn't coming.

When I heard their mother's voice again, I thought some-one was cutting down a tree – thick creak of timber. How different she sounded. So different I didn't know it was her, not even when she said her name. Even looking her in the face, I thought *It can't be her, it can't be the same woman.* But no one else speaks and moves like that, body and words keeping rhythm. The tilt to her hips, her speech a series of bursts.

She's kept her way of asking questions in the order of what it is she most wants to know with nothing extra either side. When I saw her looking around for them – I wish I'd thought to look away. Her face, when she realized.

4

Where are the twins?

Did you see the jellyfish?

What about Koan?

And then the both of us finding a way to ask one another the same question:

When did *you* realize?

The truth, the lie. The space between them.

And yes: the jellyfish. Telling us things we thought only Koan could know. A sign so clear we didn't need him there to translate. Still – when I first saw them it was Koan's voice I heard, saying words like *realignment, recalibration.*

And in my own voice, the words

'Maybe not so doomed.'

I wonder if we'd have been able to see them for what they are, if we were still with Koan. When you live in fear the fear seeps into everything. Even the simplest things turn knotted in its shadow.

Probably it makes the most sense to start with the fear.

The fear was what strung us together, at the start – when we were thinking of ways we could all of us, *together,* keep getting up in the morning.

No. That doesn't feel enough.

Given what we did.

That won't be enough to say to them.

Anna

Tonight my hawk came close to me. Close enough to set my skin prickling with the almost-touch of her feathers. Close enough I felt lit by their high-shine. The whole night might've passed this way – on my knees in the stream's cool water, spending time with my shapely, vicious bird.

Another night I wished would go on and on, would see the sun relent the sky. But a hint of pale blue let me know she was coming. Was set to spoil the night.

Already, dawn was coming and I'd yet to check the shore. I'd been on my way there when I saw my hawk had landed – when I obeyed her: knelt.

I stood up and the water running down my shins caught the light off the sinking moon, turned the skin there silver. My hawk flew away as though the gleam had displeased her. Leaning forward and for one, two wingbeats her talons were dragging up the stream and she was followed by a trail of sparkling water.

I was still hot with being close to her and with rocking on my hand by the time I came to the shoreline.

Hot with that ripe feeling, that swollen feeling that means – though I might look unchanged on the outside – inside, I have burst. Am full of seeds and juice. So when I first saw them it was from inside my warm haze and I was sure that I'd made them – that somehow, they'd come out

6

of me. Been felled from my thighs. Nothing seemed so certain as that I had in fact burst, and my liquid pleasure had shown up in the surf to be rocked and tugged by the water.

Walking toward them, sound of a red owl's guttural coo brought me out of my stupor and I could see them for what they were: supple, syrupy bodies – full, round and pulsing under the still-visible moon. Not a part of my body. A different kind of animal. A creature all their own.

If Mother was here she'd tell me their name. Like when the whales washed up, like the first time we saw a wolf cub, a garter snake or a moose. First, she'd ask us what we thought the thing should be called. Said there was something to be learned in the difference between the two sounds, that each came out of a different kind of looking.

Standing there, watching them nudge together, ease apart, I said aloud to the coastline

– Soft-Belly-Ooze.

That was how they seemed to me. The soft skin skimmed off Mother's belly a thousand times over and left to float in the surf.

And then, something about it all: making my pulse quicken. My heart and my breath no longer in time.

Remembering it fresh, again.

Mother is gone.

Mother is gone and I will never know what to call this animal.

Storm will have come, and I won't know its true name.

Our mother left in the night and we found the stain she'd made in the morning. I covered it with a rug when Koan came looking for her, which some days feels like a dignity

7

she shouldn't have been afforded. Old stain that's stuck bright on the wood.

Two years since she left and most days I have to kneel down with the panging hurt of it. Even a few moments of forgetting she's gone are enough for the remembering to move like a blade. Swift and precise, drawn to your most precious part. Some much-needed organ. And so: I have to make sure I am in a constant state of knowing – the ongoing ache of knowing is easier to hold than the pincer-shock of remembering. An ache I carry into my sleep. Not even in my dreams do I allow her, for a single moment, to return.

For a few moments after she left, before I realized her red had come, it seemed most likely she'd caught an edible animal and brought it inside. Brought it inside and upstairs, where no one would see her kill it and make her feel obliged to share.

Never mind she'd left me in the woods, or that Adam was ten feet away, asleep in the bed.

That should give you a sense of our mother.

At first, what seemed most likely – she'd put her mothering aside to take an animal upstairs, and kill it.

Adam will still sometimes ask what the stain could be. For almost a whole year he'd convinced himself it was her bleed and I told him what I knew: a stain that size from that part of the body would have been a long time in the making. More time than Mother had ever stayed still any-where. I didn't have the stomach to say, outright, *Adam, her red came. What else could possibly have happened? What else could it mean other than our mother did something she shouldn't have?*

Maybe with her hands, maybe with her mouth. That

part we couldn't know. Only that she did a thing she shouldn't have done, and it changed her.

If Koan had seen the stain, that's what he'd have said. *I knew it!* He'd say *I always knew.*

That and

Eula always had the mark of a red woman.

Russet smear, scarlet pool.

Three reasons I kept it hidden. To save Mother the shame of Koan knowing and to deny him the pleasure of saying those words aloud. And also – Adam. He has to come to know in his own time that he had a red mother. Though there are days when I think, if I'd known years would go by without him accepting it, I'd never have pulled that rug across the floor. Would have let Koan see it, and found a way to comfort my brother.

Her leaving was a way of loving us. If she'd stayed we'd have been living with another mother, a mother it would have hurt us to know.

The effort it takes him, to look at this stain and not see what it holds. An effort that takes its toll.

Some mornings when I get home and he hasn't come down yet, hasn't tended to the fire, I know it's because he's upstairs in the bedroom. Lying next to that circle on the floor. Speaking to it like it can hear him. Laughing, whispering – a closeness of the kind Mother rarely allowed. His fingers light on the ridged wood. If that stain were a puddle he'd drink from it. He'd put his lips to the wet wood and gulp.

I think of Mother killing animals in front of us and saying it was a lesson, a lesson we'd never learn if we looked away. One of the lessons I often forgot when it came to her.

Forget still, when it comes to Adam. It was a false comfort, she said, to look at the pebbled earth or the sprouting trees. Said

– You can look away but the little slaughter is still happening.

And

– Your eyes can only save you so much knowing.

By which she meant scent and sound keep coming.

– As you get older you'll know it from fifty feet, the rustle and whiff of a wasting.

Mother and her turns of phrase, when it came to killing.

Wasting.

Little slaughter.

Coming back to the cottage I know, these new animals in the surf – something else I won't tell him.

It'd put a strain on both of us, his worry and his questions.

My brother who looks at everything but sees so little.

My brother who knows only what he wants to know.

Adam

It's dawn, so we are kneeling, waiting for the sun to rise.

It's dawn, so alongside the hard feeling of stone-under-knee there's the dewy damp and the pale yellow criss-cross of first light on trees.

It's dawn, so I am wakeful and Anna is tired; it's my turn to work, hers to sleep.

Since we were children this has been the pattern of our days.

We look out over the low hills and down toward the sea where the sun is rising. When we were children I thought that every sunrise the yellow-white disc came up out of the waves, leaving the water hot and rocking behind. I thought it stayed high just long enough for the waves to turn cool, so as not to steam the whole ocean away. I can't remember what age I was when Mother told me *No, that's a trick of your vision*. This is how we grew up: living inside a mistake until someone told you otherwise, and then living inside the shadow the mistake had made.

My hand warms the back of Anna's neck and hers does the same to mine. Our faces point down but our eyes look up and it gets to hurt, after a time. Already I feel too keenly the bones in my back, the cords of muscle stiffening. That stretch-feeling in the eyes that, when we stand again, we'll try to ease with rubbing.

With your knees on the ground and
your eyes in the clouds;
this is how we call to Storm;
how we stave off carmine.

Without turning, careful not to move at all, I ask her
– Was it a long night?
– Not especially.
Though she came back with the shotgun spent.
She asks me
– And you? How'd you sleep?
– Well.
Through her nose comes a light huffing – an agreeable
sound.

And now: the sun. For a moment my child memory takes
hold and I wonder why we don't see the steam it makes on
the water.

We wait 'til it has risen gold and clear and high and
then, together,

– Come, Storm, we are waiting. We are waiting, Storm,
come.

Whenever we make devotion each of us holds tight to
the other's neck, tight enough to feel the veins bouncing.

All it takes is a sliver of crimson, cherry, cardinal or puce –
keep your red heart at bay, keep your red mouth shut tight:
you don't want Storm to forget you.

Anna and I are twins because of red, because
All burdens are less between a pair.

Inside of Mother we were single and uniform, but her body knew if we stayed whole we wouldn't survive.

And so; we divided. And the division saved us.

To be twinned is to dilute vermilion,
see it watered down to harmless pink.

If you are a twin, your red cannot take hold.

Once twinned, you're more likely to survive heartbreak and hunger; any displeasure at all has double the flesh to slip inside, meaning I take on Anna's hurt and she takes on mine.

Mirror sister.

Precious kin.

Before we were born, we'd each of us saved the other.

Every time we look at one another this is what we're seeing: what saved us, how we'll keep on living 'til Storm comes and the world reassembles; no more red, our separation undone.

I make our morning meal, throwing pieces of rabbit on to a pan over the fire.

The weather's yet to fully turn so I keep my chair close to the heat, drag it on its legs which are buffed smooth from the constant to and fro across these flat grey stones. The stones themselves are rimmed with moss, because – despite the hot earth beneath us – the moss grows everywhere, doubly thick in parts of the cottage where it's especially cool. The cottage is filled with things that once caught light and made shine but all crack and fracture, now, our cups and bowls. Our clothes and sheets wear the fact of their thread. And everything, *everything* carrying the thick smell of salt, a smell made crisp with ice in winter and come summer baked hard with sunshine heat. The cupboards are filled with it; bowls and cups and jars. Salt and salt and salt that we collect from the sea whenever its waves settle in a hard crusted foam. The wood in the kitchen is warped and flaking with all the salt it holds. The little room under the stairs that lead to our bedroom; in there we keep salt spread across the floor. It's a place for us to lie down if we ever feel a red thought coming. A place you can stuff your mouth with strips of salted linen. It's not so much a rule as a promise between us; if one of us goes in there, the other won't ask why.

Other than that – salting, sleeping, shelter – we barely use the cottage.

Some things I suspect we don't use properly, or are meant to be used another way. Some things you can tell were once marked with writing, but the letters have worn down to leave behind a kind of code.

We never use the kitchen or the bathroom, even though from spring through summer the taps will often sputter water. Like the rest of the cottage its walls are white with time passing rather than from being clean. Hard to keep anything clean with the soil one moment so damp and the next so warm; *jungle earth*, Koan once called it – *ever-seeding*.

> *This land needs constant tending;*
> *the red gets in when you let things slip –*
> *quick as a blink you'll turn sanguine.*

Koan used to say the fire beneath us was because of Storm, that we lived on a stretch of land that had soaked up her fury, but Mother told us *Koan just wants you fretting. It's an old strip mine that got set alight.*

As was often the way; one question came out of another.

– What's a strip mine?

– A caveful of coal.

– What's coal?

– Something fire loves to chew on.

Whatever coal is, there must be a lot of it beneath us because the fire burns and burns. The *sound* it makes – rocks coming down a mountain. Whenever you hear that sound you know you're standing somewhere you shouldn't be, that the earth underneath you has worn thin.

There are places where the heat off the fire kills the trees and turns them white, and other places where it's mixed with minerals so that the plants grow lush and strange. We wash the ground over with clay wherever we see these orange patches – these bursts are the only hints we have as to where and how quick the fire is moving.

Clay is soft, clay is cooling.

We're meant to rush with clay if we see even an ember, which of course we don't always. And we're not meant to breathe in the smoke it makes, which of course we often do. It comes up in grey bursts, rainclouds too close to the ground. Often, when you first see it – impossible to tell if it's steam or smoke.

Mother used to say we'd grow hooves so our soles wouldn't scorch.

Hot earth. Smell of the ground when it's sizzling.

Some mornings when I wake I see my sleep-breath has

left a grey smudge on the pillow; smoke that I took inside and that came back out while I was dreaming.

I don't mind the smudges so much as the smell.

These last few years, no matter what it is I dream of, my dreams always smell of fire.

This time of year with the days stretching out sees the nights cropped short and so Anna works less, sleeps longer.

As children we both slept out the night and spent the days together but then, when we were almost grown, turned out Anna was like Mother, meaning she got along better with the night. Before long she had her shadow-proof eyes and her skin had forgotten the light. Now she can't stand anything but the weakest sun, and if she stays out even a few moments too long she starts to blister 'cross her collar and down her throat, around her mouth. Her mouth that I once licked clean, and still sometimes put my lips to while she's sleeping, her chest and neck flushed with heat, her hands curling around some weapon that in her dream she wields.

Every night I'm sorrowful I don't get to lie beside her the whole night through, as when we were children, her stomach on my back and her face in my neck. My sister in those moments as close to me as she can be before Storm has come.

One body two hearts – apart but keeping time.

Nothing but breath between us.

Koan
Vol. 1
#1

His wife brought him in. She said he'd caught it off the cat.

She knows Matthew somehow, probably through Tabatha, and so felt comfortable walking through the building, asking people where she might find him.

I came across them quite by chance. I'd been attending a meeting on the far side of town, and now the pleasure of an uninterrupted day was unfurling before me. I had time, at last, to sit with our latest findings: the pigmentation that has been surfacing in the coats of mammals, both wild and domestic. A lush discolouration we have been considering through every rubric: virus, parasite, mutation. That, and certain phenomena, have been happening too frequently while others are in notable decline – events that were entirely cyclical but that never failed to startle. A perfect example, the blooms of jellyfish coursing up along the surf. That was something people always fixated on, invertebrate species conducting their internal culling on an annual basis. But for a time, now, almost two years, the coastlines have been mostly vacant. There has been some speculation that the sea is finding other ways to cleanse herself, but it's more likely anything that lives in the sea knows, for whatever reason, to keep away. One of the assistants had been gathering these documents together when I left that morning and this is where I was heading; to my office, to its shut door, to the neat pile of papers I would find there.

Instead I came across Matthew and this frazzled woman with her coat falling off her shoulder and her mouth moving full steam. When he looked up and saw me over the top of her head I thought he might sing with relief.

– Here he is now – the man in charge.

His voice tinny with false cheer.

The woman turned around. Busy face, close features. Watery eyes. She started talking about her husband, her husband who was sick and who someone had escorted to one of our smaller rooms.

She said she'd taken him to the doctor but that the doctor had proved 'useless',

– Absolutely useless, didn't know what he was looking at.

Then she started on about the cat while Matthew straightened the rolled-up sleeves of his shirt. It was too hot because, as always, someone had overestimated how much heat was sufficient to keep out the vicious chill of the morning. She said the cat had been 'up in the bed with him' and the next morning 'he was coming up red' around his mouth, his bottom lip so inflamed it looked like his mouth stretched 'all the way to his chin'.

It is not unusual for people to mistake the nature of my work, of this department, and come to us with items startling only for their tedium. And so, my first question was

– An allergy, surely?

In response to which, over her shoulder, I could see Matthew very gently, very slightly, shake his head.

– No sir, not an allergy. We've had that cat since it was

18

a kitten and he's never so much as sneezed. No, the cat must've got sick with something while it was outside.

Matthew's eyes on mine. *Ah*, I thought, *I see*. Another sample. To this woman I said

– How's the cat?

– Maybe it ate something, I don't know. Maybe it caught some sort of virus—

– But how's it behaving?

– What's that?

– How's the cat behaving?

She shrugged her shoulders inside her coat. Looked at a notice about tics on the wall. A notice whose information is outdated as tics have been growing steadily, the last few years. No need of torchlight, now, to spot them.

– She's been licking herself.

– Cleaning herself, you mean?

– No.

That shrugging again that did nothing other than raise the collar of her coat to her jaw which the cheap cloth had already pinkened.

– Not cleaning. *Licking*. She has a sore spot on her leg and she's licking it. The one spot, over and over.

Again, I looked at Matthew. Yes. Something we had been dealing with, something we had seen before. Not this exactly, but its kin.

– She has a sore?

– Well, a red patch of skin. If it's not a sore I don't know what it is. But this is what I'm telling you. The cat has a sore and so does my husband.

Trying to think clearly there in the corridor. The hum of the heating, this woman's moist breath.

19

– And your husband.

– His lips are—

– Yes, his lips are red. Anything else?

– Only that . . . he's making sounds.

– Sounds.

She said nothing else, only looked behind her at Matthew, who gazed over his crossed arms at the floor.

– But he's not in pain? Not agitated or alarmed?

– No, no, no. If anything he seems – I don't know.

Sharp suck of breath: I thought she might cry, the way she moved her hand around her head. Like she was at the salon, conveying agitation at her hair's lacklustre shine.

– He seems very calm.

This woman in her awful coat, Matthew with his eyes disappeared into the cast shadow of his brow. The clock on the wall told me it was a quarter to ten in the morning. What time could she and her husband have woken? Seven? Eight? And already they'd been to the doctor and made their way here, having realized the doctor was insufficient. She'd wasted no time. She didn't know what we knew, about what we'd been seeing, accruing. But still: she was panicking. And about what, exactly, she had yet to say.

– Well, I said, let's go see him.

From a pump on the wall I rubbed my hands over with stringent foam and we began walking to the end of the corridor. Behind me I heard Matthew ask the woman her husband's name.

Such are the ways he is useful to me. He cares as little as I do for these details but, when necessary, he creates an *illusion* of caring.

When we got to the door, the woman stopped: went so

20

far as to touch my arm with her square fingers. She'd been pressing and pressing, and now that we were here, where she wanted us to be, she was stalling.

– You have to understand, my husband . . .

Tall Matthew stood behind her: looking straight down at the top of her head. He could not see what I was seeing, which was something very familiar to me. What fear can do to a person's face, how it further deepens the already creased features of the ageing and elderly.

– My husband is usually . . . a very proper kind of person.

Anna

Was a time Koan was always telling me to brace myself for the night-time woods, for their red hurt and their red terror. But as soon as I was inside them I could hear the tree bark and the gorse, the streambed winnowing.

The woods are different once dipped in velvet dark and that's what it feels like, passing through them at night – like it's velvet you're wading through.

By then I'd been a long time garnering my night-time eyes so I could walk almost quickly, almost steadily, and I knew the woods wanted me there. Were moments I felt them part to let me move deeper inside them. And all the slick, hungry creatures – the owls with their cherry eyes and the snakes with their garnet bellies – they knew, too, that I should be there.

I don't know if this feeling is a red feeling come out of my red womb or red heart, I only know I feel it like I feel nothing else – the woods and their dark and their singing.

Strange that now it's just us and Koan when I don't think he ever said our names out loud 'til Mother was gone. Even though we spent all that time with him for our lessons, hours and hours in his house. A pair of specimens that, because of how and when we were born, might tell him something new. Turned out this wasn't the case, and so he lost interest in us as we got older. But for a while Adam kept going to see him. After devotion he'd go straight there with a bowl of food. I thought it was because he was lonely during the day, with Mother and me sleeping. Or maybe I thought Koan was trying to treat his eye, the sudden pinprick of black that flared up around that time. The type of small sickness Koan could usually stop spreading. Then he didn't go one, two, three days in a row, and I never thought much about why until the others left. *Had* to start thinking about why, because almost right away Koan turned old and sickly.

They left a little under a year after Mother and it was like they'd timed it, or like he'd been waiting for them to go. Overnight he was a man with a shake in his hands and a head too heavy for his neck. Either way, with them gone and him sick, who else was going to feed him? Light his fire? There was only us left, but Adam would not go. Face flat and still as a plank of wood whenever I asked him. And so for a year it's been up to me to bring him his food. Make sure he's warm. Keep him living until Storm.

And Koan, for his part, never asks after Adam.

I think maybe they were both hit too hard by the others going away. I think for Adam it brought back Mother disappearing, the sight of them leaving – more than she ever gave us, the chance to watch her go. But all the same: that severing feeling. And Koan. Well. He'd tried to make them stay and they'd gone anyway. Didn't matter what he did and didn't know, how close he was to Storm. They'd stopped caring what he wanted. His words counted for nothing, and it ruined him.

If Mother could see us: Adam's eye still getting worse, and Koan getting less and less like Koan.

23

Both of them suckling on me, hungry for the comfort of another breathing body.

Tonight, once the treeline had taken me: my throat came open and breath rushed my every part. The woods washing me clean of Koan's twitching mouth and Adam's sick vision – not just cleaning me but bathing me, moving a cloth over my shoulders, lifting my hair up from my neck so that the night air could land and make cool there.

Fresh night, still and viscous.

The trees only every so often creaking and making me think of winter when they tighten and buckle within their cases of ice and snow. The whole wood loud with a neighing sound you might mistake for horses. The red wolves calling out. Whisper of a track the red deer leave behind.

The woods and the gifts they give me. At the very bottoms of hills and at the very tops of trees. Kneeling in the stream and seeing my hawk, who always knows when and where to come for me. I first saw her after Mother left, and she's not reddened an inch in all that time.

Mother once said the kind of hawk she is was always a bit red. We saw one out in the woods and she said

– That's a breed that carries its red in the tail.

I know my hawk will still be whole and full, when Storm arrives. I know she'll sit in her tree and watch Her coming, unsurprised. Enjoy the gathering wind that sets her feathers rustling.

My hawk: a creature that will always be there.

Immaculate. Irreplaceable.

Immovable as stone.

*

Those creatures are still there.

Some of them in the surf looking smudged and faded.

Some of them still shining in the sea.

Still enough of them that the water itself is thickening, has slowed – the light a burden it's grown tired of reflecting.

Veil-like, just under the surface of the water, moving there like some cautious animal nosing its way through the brush.

And inside each of them an orb that flashes purple, red and green depending on the tilt of the sea.

Adam

A horse and cart comes down the road.

Not the main road, but the back road. That thin clay road that cuts between two fields and has its edges threaded with little red buds now that it's springtime. Another season come overnight.

There are two children in the cart. They each wear a coarse white shirt and a pair of grey trousers with the pleat's curt fold long fallen out of shape.

I'm keeping watch, kneeling in the long grass and watching the back of Anna's head, the long barrel of the shotgun and its whistling gleam. I know without looking the mark it leaves on her shoulder – pink, soft. Her hair is the same colour as the field because we've gone fifteen days with no rain. Dry, dry grass, though in places it sparkles with dew.

If I see anything or anyone creeping toward us I'm to call out, one time, and then run back to the cottage.

In front of me, on the ground: bucket of salt. Its glittering dust piled high.

The horse and cart is almost level with us now, which means that Anna will soon see their faces clearly. The cart's wheels are loud and grating on the splintered pebbles of the road. From this distance I can already see that the horse is old, and not particularly large. Maybe it was born into its smallness, or has been a long time underfed.

Closer and closer and Anna is waiting and waiting. Slight slouch to her shoulders which she often has when she is making ready to do something she doesn't want to do.

I know what she'll be saying to herself. It's the same thing I'm saying. Between our two heads the one thought pulsing, which is *There's always a chance.*

A chance they might not be red.

What will happen if she doesn't need to shoot them? Her shoulders will straighten, settle with letting go a breath deeply held. They'll never know we saw them, that they were watched by a brother and sister who live in a cottage less than half a mile away from this slight bend in the road – they'll just keep on going with their small horse into the brightening day.

Closer, closer and closer again.

Wheels at uneven angles to the uneven road.

Grate of metal.

Creaking as their bodies rock against the wood.

Anna's shoulders.

The gun quiet and grey, her ear dipped toward it like it's speaking, whispering low. Once I put my own ear against it to hear what Anna spends so much of her time hearing and sure enough: a rushing sound. A shoreline sound.

There, on the back of her neck. Sweat beading. Her body showing its fear in this thick, salted juice.

Again, I picture the cart passing us, Anna's shoulders softening. But the fear is too much. The chance of their redness. A carmine gush of loud and angry water. I think of green, which is the opposite of red. Endless green. Green leaves, green hills. I shut my eyes and picture these children, who cannot be more than fifteen, with emerald lashes. I pretend they've come to tell us that red is done, it's been overcome by sage and olive.

I open my eyes when the shot rings out, see the girl fall into the boy's lap. The crackle is loud in the dawn. Too loud for the day's first sound. From underneath the crackle I hear Koan, his voice ringing out with the clear glass sound it had when we were children: *The red man can taste you from ten feet away. He means to be inside you, or to take you inside himself.*

Now the boy turns his spattered face toward us and his cheeks are round, flushed, his nose freckled. Another shot, ringing, and they are both slumped now, one over the other.

Your every part he'll try to take in his mouth: the red man is fixed on a union with any other flesh.

The reins have not fallen from the boy's hands and the horse carries on down the path, step after step, the two small bodies slumping in time with his tread.

He'll lie down beside you and tell you it won't hurt, that at most it'll only tingle.

The horse didn't bolt. The horse must be deaf.

Anna stands, clearing the grass, and walks toward the cart. She takes long steps and when she gets close to the horse it stops and lets out one steaming, haggard breath. Relieved of her gun her shoulder keeps its mark; when we were young the skin there always seemed close to tearing, but she has a callus of sorts there now, in her shoulder's crook.

Her whole body: a series of calluses.

A string of wounds hurried into healing.

I walk quickly, before the grass can close behind her. The bucket pulls on my arm, the muscle which joins my shoulder and my neck.

She's standing very close to the cart and the deaf horse and the dead children. Aside from the blood and the hurt on her face the girl might be fallen into a dreamy stupor across her brother's knees and he, with the strange angling of his limp arms, might be considering how to move without waking her.

Both of them pale, and both of their heads topped with a bunch of dark, unruly hair. Their white shirts soaking up the blood. Their eyes wide open, their ears deeply rimmed with maroon. Their noses, too, stained with rust. These things Anna sees from a distance, before they've come too close to do us damage.

She hoists her gun back on to her shoulder. The sun is only beginning to colour the sky.

– Adam? Are you all right?

I look at her in the peachy light.

– They were brother and sister, I say.

She looks away, her jaw hardening. She hears what I don't say out loud: *Brother and sister, probably born no more than a year apart but still, their red came through.*

Born so close they might have passed one another coming out of the womb.

Close, but not close enough.

Anna has put her hand flat on her chest which is how she cries. I don't know if I've ever seen her eyes let loose their water but too many times I've seen her press her hand against herself and train her vision on the floor, measuring the jolt of her heart. I can feel the pressure of her palm as though I'm stretched thin beneath it. I'm the film of sweat that pools in the divot of her collarbone. The tears she keeps at bay, salty veil behind her eyes.

29

She reaches toward me, reaches for the bucket. I turn my face 'til my bad eye covers the sight but it cannot cover the sound. The salt rushing on to their faces where it'll burn, purify.

– What do you see, Adam?

– Raincloud, coming heavy over mountain.

I hear her climb on to the cart, I hear her pat the horse on its haunch.

Small mercy: no red. The horse can go unshot.

Maybe we'll be beneath that cloud when it decides to burst.

– What else?

– Tall tree, branches thin.

On and on: the salt rushing.

– What else?

– The long grass . . . It's yellow, not green.

The handle squeaks which means the bucket is swinging the way it only does when it's empty.

– And?

– The thistle growing prickly and thick.

The sound of her feet back on the ground. Of something being dragged to the side of the road.

– Anything else?

– The cottage. I can see our cottage.

And I can. I can see its unused chimney stack, the hard angle of the roof's very tip.

– All right.

I don't turn around. Anna has untethered the horse and I feel the damp heat of it come close to me. When she leads it in front of us I see its muzzle is flecked silver and grey. I climb on to its back and Anna leads us by the reins into the grass, my hips moving in time to his steps while his mane sparkles between my thighs.

– That wasn't too bad.

– No. Not so bad today.

Meaning we didn't have to shoot the horse or hear anything those red children had to say.

But we must be quick, now, so that we don't miss the sun reaching her perch in the sky.

Every morning it rises and sees us a little different, a little more tired and impatient than the day before.

And so it always seems a foreign sun.

It seems we've a new sun every day.

With devotion done we rub one another over with salt in our understairs room.

It gathers in a pile against the skirting every time we open the door and we smooth it out again with our hands and our feet, squat and make quick scuffing circles on one another's chest and shoulders. Anywhere the red might have touched. For a day like today with the children on the road we need only salt one another 'til we feel a mild stinging. They were only close to us after they had died, and so there's no need for salt under the tongue, inside the ears. No need to dab at the corners of our eyes.

Anna goes to feed Koan, comes back and eats quickly so the meat's juice trails pink 'round her wrist. She uses the back of her hand to wipe her eyes and says goodnight, goes upstairs. But almost right away she's back again, her dress off and her hair down. She says

– The dew.

Grey half-moon shapes under her eyes.

31

– The dew in the grass.

I nod: *Yes, I saw, I know.*

– The red buds by the road.

Why is she telling me something I already know – that the seasons are changing?

– It's our birthday.

She means some time this month, this first part of the new season. We've no way of knowing the day.

I look down to the hills, into the trees, as if something about the morning light washing over the woods will confirm the fact of us ageing.

We hold one another.

A kiss on the mouth, a kiss on each cheek.

Another year gone.

No doubt she thought the news would warm me but it spoils my day. Impossible to think of our birthday without thinking about how much time has passed. Twenty-one years since we were born into the farrow room. Twenty-one years of bruised-knee and bent-neck devotion.

Twenty-one years we've been waiting.

Two years without our mother, with only the stain she left behind that Anna every so often rubs her foot over.

A stain made by our mother.

The stain Mother made.

Mother's stain.

Sometimes I pretend it's her mucus and blood, a mark she made while birthing. I picture her overcome by our birth and not making it to the farrow room, not even making it to her own bed.

Or: simply deciding she didn't want the later trouble of

cleaning the sheets in the stream and so lying down on the floor. Not even a pillow for her back, her head.

Our strong, strong mother. Mostly woman but also iron, also stone.

I'd rather her there on the floor than the farrow room, where she'd have been just like any other mother whose time had come.

On her back, needing the help of others.

And most likely Koan squatting between her parted legs.

Another year gone, but Storm is close. I feel Her closeness when I eat and sleep and wring out the sheets in the stream. My blood pumps smoother when I dream of Storm and being returned to my sister. The hair on the back of her neck, the soft bedding beneath her fingernails, the quick loose flesh under her tongue like the torn gullet of a hare; a place very soft, and rarely seen.

Koan
Vol. 1
#2

The first off thing was that he didn't turn around. He'd sat himself with his back to the door and when I opened it he stayed just so; sitting up on the table. And so I took him in from behind. Greying hair, recently cut into a neat V down his neck, stopping just above his shirt's crisp collar. Most likely he was a man who'd worked and worked until they told him it was time to spend his days at home, but he never got out of certain habits. Could never abide a crumpled shirt.

As I moved around him I could see the dark coat folded in his lap. Could see his hands, his forearms. His muscles had kept their shape beneath the tissuey, ageing skin. I moved slowly and looked at his chest, shoulders, his neck with the barest hint of silver gristle. This was probably the first morning for many mornings that he'd gone without shaving. Then: his face. A pleasing broadness to his jaw, his nose. A ruddy warmth to his cheeks; often in the sun, but rarely burned. A man who took to water on his weekends and squinted at the white foam on the waves. All of this – the neat narrative of his life contained in his clothes, his face – was entirely at odds with the lurid red of his mouth which did indeed seem to envelop the lower half of his face. Wet and shining and surely immensely, distractingly painful. I thought *This woman is mad, her husband has lost the skin of his chin to a burn.*

– Sir, hello – are you in pain?

By now I was standing where I could look at him fully. His chest rising, measured and slow.

– Your wife has brought you in because she's worried about this sore on your mouth.

I could see his pulse inside the open flesh of his chin. Thinking suddenly of the landscape of my childhood, come spring. Topsoil sheathed away.

– She tells me you've been to the doctor?

The woman was nodding now, staring at the back of her husband's head. Matthew was standing with his back to the door, blocking it, as though someone in the room were likely to bolt.

– And the doctor could not help you?

This time, on 'doctor', he flinched a little.

Transparent hair at his temples. By his complexion and eyes I could imagine the dark-brown hair of his youth.

– Can you tell me anything about how you're feeling?

I raised my fingers to my own chin and he blinked, now, in a way that struck me as purposeful.

– How about I say some words to you, and you let me know, with your eyes, if I've said something that rings true?

Again: slow blink, and his eyes sparking bright when the lids came up again.

– All right, then.

The wife nodding, the shut door behind Matthew's back.

– Your chin is burning.

Nothing.

– Your chin is stinging.

Nothing.

– Your chin is aching.

Nothing.

– Your chin is pounding.

Again, nothing, and what made me say what I said next I'm not sure. Perhaps it was because I was struggling for another appropriate term. Perhaps because his back was so straight it seemed he was leaning against something I could not see. Perhaps it was his eyes, their fevered brightness.

– Your chin is tingling.

Sure enough, at this, inside this open sore, this wound, his lips commenced twitching. I thought *He's trying to speak to me but his voice is weakened*, and so I stepped closer.

– Your chin is pulsing.

Now, it seemed he realized his tongue was failing him, and so he involved the muscles of his throat.

– Stroking.

His shoulders, too, now moving like the words were pieces of food he had to work back up from his stomach. I stepped closer again, said

– Lick.

His chest, which had before moved silently, now jerked like there was a rodent in his shirt.

And then I was hearing it.

Right away, I knew for the rest of my life there wouldn't be some part of me that wasn't always hearing it. That if I wasn't hearing it in my ears I'd be hearing it in my heart, my gut. The sound this man had started to make.

This man with his torn mouth, purring.

36

The tongue itself possessed with a vibratory hum, a quiver deep in the muscle.

The wife's hands were near her throat.

Doctor didn't know what he was looking at.

– Do you hear it? Can you hear it?

He caught it off the cat.

– All morning he's been doing it. I woke up and turned over and he was there with the cat on his chest and the two of them purring—

The man rolled his head back and opened his mouth at the ceiling and still the terrible sound: constant, cruel, soft and coy. There was a blush moving up his neck: blood freshly warmed by the rotations of his large heart.

He'll never be able to use his tongue for anything else. It'll fail him in speech, in taste. And another part of me, which I pushed away, said *This ruined mouth his wife once knew from kissing.*

The wife who was begging him now, saying

– Adrian, stop that, stoppit Adrian—

And, as the moments wore on and his cheeks produced teardrops of sweat, only

– Please, Adrian, *please.*

Then he did stop, and it seemed for a moment we'd misread everything entirely – nothing so serious it couldn't be halted with a tired wife's pleading. But the purring had stopped because his heart had stopped, which was clear from the way he dropped to his side. The slack weight of his body pulling him to the ground, his upper body swaddled by the shirt which the wife had probably ironed. Probably neither of them ever settled fully into the new routine of his

37

retirement. Probably they'd spent his career making all sorts of plans for when they had the time to travel, but had found reasons to put it off for another month or week or day until they found themselves here, in this room, with two strange men.

The wife's weeping, somewhat surprisingly, didn't waver in rhythm even as she went to him and began to touch him all over. We'd only been in the room a few minutes, but I think she'd been saying goodbye to her husband from that first moment in the bedroom this morning. I think she'd woken up and seen, in the bed beside her, a creature she did not recognize.

I looked at Matthew, who'd gone quite pale. Over his shoulder, on one of the shelves in the corner – a textbook I'd been missing for some time whose cover picked up the artificial light in a garish way.

I'm sure there was plenty, in that moment, he wished that I would say. I don't think he would have cared if it was the most unfounded extrapolation, the most outrageous lie, but he looked at me in such a way I knew he only wanted me to speak some false comfort that would, even if only for a moment, dull the sound of this woman weeping. I said

– Go on, Matthew.

By which I meant *Go and make the necessary calls.*

Looking back on it now it was telling – that neither of us tried to resuscitate the man, tried to comfort the wife.

Matthew said

– Do we need assistance?

Which was a code of sorts for *Should I ring the alarm?*

– No, there's no need.

Which there wasn't. It was forming before me now: this

38

was not a matter of virus or contagion. At least, not in the usual way. He posed us no threat, having died.

The wife had lain across him, was clinging to her his body and kissing him everywhere. A person walking in at this moment might think it was her kisses that had ravaged his face.

– What will I tell the others?

– Nothing, for now. Let none of them in this room.

Matthew putting his body at an angle so that he could leave without fully opening the door. The wife, at my feet, had raised one leg partly around the body. Between the line of her raised skirt and her stocking: streak of white, dimpled thigh.

Watching her keen there on the floor I wished she would pull her skirt down, put that skin away.

Anna

Though I'd rather the others hadn't left, rather I didn't have to spend so much time with sickly Koan, one good thing – I get to read his journals.

Not every time, but most times when I take him a meal, he gets distracted with his own ramblings. He talks and talks and I go right up to the bookcase where their bindings are pressed close in an even line. Each one is the same pale-brown colour with the same number of pages inside.

It took me a while to figure out certain words, and it was strange to read that many lines one after another. But turns out Koan writes exact same he speaks and I've lived my whole life with his voice in my ear, so after a couple of months I started pretending the words on the page were coming out of his mouth and then everything came together.

He's lined them up in a kind of order: top left corner is when they first got here, before we were born. Bottom right corner is just before he got sick and his head and his hand fell out of time. That's the order, mostly, I've been trying to read them in. Still: some parts make less sense than others, and there are parts I don't read – where he's talking about Mother.

Today was a day he was too wound up and I couldn't get near them.

Complaining about Mother as if he'd only just seen her,

had just run into her on the woodland path where we'd sometimes hear them fighting.

– Your mother thinks about herself and no one else. That woman lives her life with her tongue on fire.

Probably she'd laugh if she knew he talks about her so often, but it gives me a cornered feeling. Mouth gagged. Ankles tied. Same trapped feeling as when we had our lessons. Hours and hours of sitting and singing, not allowed to get up or walk away. One lesson after another about Storm, about red, the red spectrum and its every variations in kind. Reciting in order of frequency and intensity which was the most startling, which more likely to spread, which the more ominous sign.

– What reds are weak reds?

– Crimson, carmine, scarlet, puce.

– What reds are hurtful reds?

– Vermilion, ruby.

– What reds are carnal?

– Cochineal, cerise and sanguine.

On and on reciting patterns and shades, like he was trying to plant dreams inside our heads. Like he wanted to know what we were seeing even while we slept.

One of the first things we learned: red man's caul. How a body wears its red. Koan said it shows where your body betrayed you to the world, those places where the flesh is weak, *is aperture*. Probably the boy and girl this morning heard something they weren't supposed to. Listening deeply to something they shouldn't have and the listening gave them pleasure, and so that's where their caul came through.

Mother didn't like it when we said caul. Said it was something that grew with a baby and that Koan should have picked another word. There were other words that fitted, and when we were with her it was those words we tried to use.

You're not long for the world, once your red veil starts falling.

Finally the food was gone and I could take the bowl.

Sound of him spitting Mother's name on to the floor as I closed the door.

Though he loved to fight with Mother, all Koan ever had to do was turn quiet if he wanted to get his way. Only had to give the impression of noticing something, and keeping it to himself. This was enough to start people panting, make them wild with panicky thirst. And if someone said or did something Koan didn't like he could go quiet for days, and everyone would start seeing their own signs everywhere.

I saw a patch of red soil just off the track.

The stream's running the wrong way.

Either the birds were too quiet or there were too many fox calls come night-time.

No matter how many times he did it, no one recognized it as a trick he played.

And it worked, it brought people to heel. I remember someone begging Mother not to say anything that might anger him, saying *He's only just started back speaking.* I used to think it was entirely effortless; the withholding. But then, no one ever so loved the sound of their own voice, so it must have cost him something.

Coming into the woods and their ring of early springtime.

Running past a fresh pocket of embers, and nearby

another patch of ground that's started smoking. Each hot hole only the size of a footprint so they can wait 'til morning. No rush when they're still feet-size.

Adam can come, after devotion, and tend to them – can sweep each of them over with clay.

Our birthday. Another year.

Not so long a time, when you think how long that fire's been burning.

Not so long to have been sister to a sick brother.

Still. The whole night I keep thinking I see him. When I see my hawk, when I see cautious moonlight strike the water. When I see anything that gives me pleasure he appears; shadow twin. Not the first time it's happened and always the same feeling. Rope 'round my throat, a feeling like I left the windows open and all night red birds have been flying inside. Snared wingbeats up in the rafters.

Down to the shore.

Maybe ten still there.

Ebbing and gathering, nudging and probing in the surf.

For the first time I kneel in the sand and look at them.

No heart, no lungs. No blood and no brain.

A look of dirty glass, the kitchen window smudged and foggy.

Faded, but still – swirl of light caught inside.

If all the longing a person ever felt were to be given substance this is what it would be – the fat drained out of a body. Ounce by ounce, washed out and laid thick on the sand.

Adam

We've kept the horse and he shares his warmth when I stand beside him. I worry about something happening to him all day, and make sure he's never too long in my bad sight. The pain so full it spills right down my neck and when we make worship Anna's grip is a palmful of pincers.

We sit down to eat and she starts talking and I forget the pain by dreaming myself inside there, the spit 'cross her tongue. Feel the swallowed water running past me, her breath coming in bursts when she runs.

She throws a cloth at me, the one I use to wipe the pot dry, says

– Wake up, brother. The daytime's starting.

And she goes around the side of the cottage, to the big house to give Koan his food, disappearing into the blur of my sick eye. When I wake up with this kind of pain I worry my red is starting to show. I worry I dreamt something unseemly, saw something I shouldn't have, and that next time I blink there'll be a cherry rim to my vision.

I clean up 'round the fire and see where Anna marked our names in the ashes while they were cooling. It's a habit of hers to put our names on this or that surface, something her body does for comfort while she's not looking. An easy pleasure; marking us down in dust or dirt, and a way to

44

think about Mother without saying her name out loud, because Mother taught us our letters in the ground. I don't know what age we were when she started – old enough to keep a secret. Letter after letter shaped in the soil, grooves filled in with pebbles worn small and smooth. Said if Koan ever caught us crouching we should say we were checking the soil for fire, told us

No harm in keeping some clay in your pocket.

She said touch was the thing you remember by and so touch was how we learned them, tracing their shape while saying their sound. I still feel it when I say a letter out loud – the shape of it under my fingers.

By the time she left she'd taught us full words but she never showed us how they might be strung together – she was always rushing, always ready to scuff away the lesson.

Deviation from the tasks at hand will thread your idle palms with claret.

But without Mother's letters in the soil we wouldn't know that flowers used to have different names and be colours other than red, or that the sun and moon are two sibling planets and not the same disc painted a different colour on each side.

We always said Mother never stood still but there were mornings when, after she'd run back here, she'd look toward the fire and wait for her breath to slow – said there was no point lying down until it was calm again.

Mother with her lessons you didn't always know were lessons.

Moments when she'd let me lean against her. She'd take off her shirt and I could fit my body into the curve of her

45

left side – my face against her waist, the bone of her hip, the damp soft of the skin there.

– You see the waves, Adam? See how they rise? Why don't you count them?

Mother loved the sea for a reason other than its salt but that was the kind of close, soft thing she wasn't in the habit of telling – why she loved a thing.

– Pick a wave, she'd say, pick a wave and track it. See how it makes its way to the shore.

Even now, the warm feeling it makes in me; counting the waves as they're cresting.

– What does a wave do?

And the answer was always the same:

– It rises.

When I remember myself on those mornings I remember myself fully grown, but of course I was still a child. I never let the memory come to its close, which is the feel of her squeezing my shoulder, stepping to the side. Just as her heat started to spread into my cold skin, that was the moment the touch was too much for her, and she had to shrug me away.

Mother; a blanket on that half of my body, constant breath on my right side.

The waves rolling forward, foaming at the seams – climbing.

One thing besides the stain that I can keep: our close bodies while she spoke those words.

Wave.

Cresting.

Rising.

*

46

I'm slow today. Slowed down by those red siblings, their faces repeating on me.

Once Storm was on Her way, anything that was born was red. Anything that wasn't a twin or an animal born into a pair, a litter.

A twin is a body with its red diffused.

This is something we never managed to get right, here: how to bring on a twinning. Not everyone is like Mother, able to control their own flesh. There was a lot the others tried. Months before the birth, for instance, if the mother had a partner the partner would steep thread in warmed milk and unspool it, slowly, on to her belly, then rub in the moisture. They used the milk of whatever animal we had nearby at the time, a cow or a mare. Koan said it helped get nutrients straight to the womb, the rubbing before and after making *porous and receptive* the skin. Other times they might take a rabbit heart and cut it in two with a warm knife, place the two slivers around the bellybutton.

Then, when the baby was coming, Koan would put a hood over the mother's head. He'd only take it off, after, if there was no hint of red. There was always a chance of twinning, even if the mother's stomach was low and small. Right up until the mother gave birth; always a chance, always. But it never happened. The mother had to lie there waiting for the hood to come off and when it didn't – well, that was how they knew. The baby wasn't going to live; Koan would stopper their breath. If the hood stayed on all they could do was lie there and listen to Koan taking the baby outside. The baby that wasn't in fact a baby but the beginnings of a very savage, very ferocious person.

Crimson-vicious.

Carmine-cruel.

The rest of us knew when we saw Koan coming out with another bundle that he took into the trees.

Sometimes the others cried or shouted or screamed. Sometimes they asked what was the point of devotion with all the children coming out alone and red, and Koan said their prayers must be half-hearted, or that the mothers themselves had somehow courted red.

She must have spoken with her red mouth, loved with her red heart.

Every time a born-red baby was put in the ground a tree was planted on top of them and often, when the wind comes that way, it carries the sound of them crying. The crying they never made, seeped out underground and grown up into these five thin trees.

I know Anna will sometimes go through there at night. She claims not to hear the sound they make but I hear it and I can't stand it. Whenever I have to go near those trees I'll put my hands flat over my ears. Worst of all is when there's a hard rain and it churns up the soil and pummels the leaves – you think you're smelling milk but it's all their tears you're smelling. Mother once called it an orchid smell. I think orchids must have been a hateful flower.

Tabatha

Stopping every so often, too often, to pat myself down.

Feeling it under my palm where I know it'll be, the slim bulk the paper made when it was folded.

How she pushed the page in front of me, said her hand was aching and she couldn't write it out another time. Not my words but in my hand. I almost wrote it out a second time seeing how unpractised some of my letters were, how poorly formed, but in the end I didn't have the stomach for it.

She kneaded herself while she watched me write it. The flesh between her hips, her groin. Of all the women, to be slowed down. She said it hurts when it comes but it's not the hurt that makes her slow, the hurt she can handle. It's the dragging feeling. Like she's pulling an old numb tail behind her.

I still felt we should go together, and told her as much. Asked her how much longer it could take, how slow could she be?

But she said no, said

– The rate I'm moving these days you'll get there ten days ahead of me.

And then back to the jellyfish, on and on about the jellyfish. We had proof, now, and she would not waste one more day.

I had to go ahead of her and I had to go now.

– You've a man to take care of your baby.

And the way she said it – I knew she wouldn't let me say no.

I had no excuses, because I had a father to match my child.

Bracing myself for the pain of moving through the trees that mark the small, makeshift graves – one of them the point at which a body I made went into the ground.

The loss of your sister still fresh these years later. It will never be anything but fresh, I know, but I thought some of the terror that came with it might have slipped away. That, and the thought that I might not have kept you. If we'd stayed, when you came I might have thought you a monster.

Would never have seen your face, your collection of perfect limbs strung 'round a perfect torso.

Even walking toward the trees seems enough to reach back and undo the sweet weight of you in my womb, the feel of you suckling on my heart. The first quiver when I knew that something precious and cellular had taken root and I said *Yes, take my heart. What use my heart, without you? Have your pick of any organ.*

I felt you everywhere: stretching the length of each calf, pooled in the backs of my knees, taut in my tendons that ached with another day spent reaching into cupboards and trees.

I felt you like a spool of thread that my hips worked to stop unravelling.

You were no cruelty that my body wanted to expel.

It was not a feeling I could live again, the feeling of

50

motherhood taken away. That's something they might understand, about why we left. That you can only live with so much cruelty. That your body can only absorb so much, whether it's all at once or over time.

Something else I don't know: what I'll do about Koan.

Though I've spent so many nights dreaming it. Since the very moment we first knew absolutely, positively and for certain. That first month after you were born; I wanted to turn around and go back the way we came.

I knew for sure, at that time. What I'd do, and how much easier I'd eat and drink and sleep and laugh once I'd done it. Seemed I was living off the dreamt pleasure of the hurt I would do to him and that alone. Not water, not meat, only the warm, spillover feeling that came whenever I dreamt his torn throat. That was what nourished me.

Easy to forget, at such a time, that any power he had we handed to him.

Handed it to him piece by piece, day by day.

The night Matthew came home and said *Something happened at work* and his lips were raw and I asked if they were sore, asked why the skin was so dry. Turned out he'd walked the whole way home in the biting cold because when he got into the car he couldn't remember how to drive it.

The night I looked out and saw a man outside our house, his hand on his thigh.

Any time we saw something that scared us it made a little more sense, what Koan was saying.

And the more we saw, the more he spoke.

There was a kind of sense to it, what he said.

Yes. A kind of sense.

Slippery and hazy, gone as soon as you looked it in the face.

But enough to hinge the fear on.

Enough to feel that some gaps, at least, were being filled.

It'll be a shock for them, to see me.

No. Shock is too weak a term.

It'll be a cruel terror, those first few minutes. When they see me and I start talking – all of it coming together at once . . . It'll be asking a lot of them.

But it can't be helped. It has to happen.

Probably they think their mother left them with nothing but I know she left them with her force, her will.

A woman whose eyes would slide through stone.

Leaving traces behind, for her children.

Seeds tucked tight in an apple's core.

Something I know to be true but cannot say: *We would not have left you, if you'd been the children of another mother.*

Koan
Vol. 1
#3

He asked me what I knew he would ask me as soon as we were alone.

– What do you think happened?

– I'm still piecing it together.

The flushed cheeks and the beads of sweat.

Symptoms pertaining to any standard inflammation of the heart.

Without the sparkling eyes and skinned chin, without the animal cadence in his throat; a heart attack of the most daily variety.

– Give me the pieces, then.

– I'd rather wait 'til it makes sense.

– Koan.

I couldn't see him because we were sitting in the dark. We'd both been sitting there in our coats, ready to leave, for some time, but with our eyes on our knees the heating had turned off and the day had ended around us.

– I'm thinking he wasn't in pain when he died.

– No.

– I'm thinking it was the opposite of pain.

– Yes.

– A kind of pleasure.

The eyes rolling back in his head. In his lap, his fingers flaring, turning his hands into a pair of stars repeatedly bursting.

– Anything else?

– She was right. He caught it off the cat. But it's not contagious. Or at least, not in the traditional way.

– On account of the wife.

– Yes. She spent the night in the bed beside him.

Thankful for the dark so that he couldn't see how I was pressing my fingers against my eyes.

– Please tell me what you're thinking, Koan, because I cannot make sense of it.

The expanded red of his mouth. The fact of the purring.

– I think he tried it.

From his side of the shadow-black room, slight rasp of his breath.

– The purring. I think he tried the purring.

The click of him swallowing.

– And I think he liked the feel of it. I think it released something in him and it came out of him. I think that's what we were seeing in that . . . substance taking over his mouth.

Maybe he was crossing or uncrossing his legs. He did something, in any case, to cause a rough chafing noise in his chair.

– What else?

– Dammit, Matthew, that's enough. You've eyes the same as mine.

I try to avoid snapping at any of them, but it can't be helped when they needle at me like children. I said to

54

myself, as always, *This is the cost of it, being in charge. This is the cost of it and it is not so much; being asked to share what you know.* I tried again.

– Like I say, I don't know yet. But something about it . . . I'm thinking it matters that his mouth was red. That deep red. And not some other colour.

Because this was the issue. This was the real crux. But it was too soon to say it, yet. What had struck me clear and bright as a bell. For now, I said only

– I think that his body was working to expel something, but couldn't. I think his mouth only showed us a trace of what was going on inside.

– Yes, I think you're right.

His tone turned cautious, working to avoid my sharp tongue, and another rustling sound which might have been him nodding. He had a scarf on. I had watched him tie it in a knot at his throat.

Now he asked me something I hadn't thought of.

– How much will you tell the others?

– Oh . . . I've yet to decide.

They had all been sent home hours ago, and as of yet they did not know why. It made me want to lie down and sleep on the floor: their confused faces.

Matthew righting himself in the chair. Thinking about the others let him get out from under his own fear, his own thoughts.

– They might chafe a little.

– Let them chafe. They'll hear what I have to say when I'm ready.

Often, I remind them they are not here by force. That they can leave and be elsewhere, seek out other tutelage. I remind them they came to me for a reason, and I can happily replace them should they choose to go away.

Together we walked outside and for the first time in hours I could see his face when we said goodbye; illuminated by the flickering, ignorant lights of the skyline. I could see it was the white-blue of very fresh milk and very bright snow.

He pulled on one end of his scarf so the knot sat higher, tighter. Rose up from his collar and sat at the dead centre of his throat. He said

– We should've known.

– All we can ever do is work with what we have at the time.

He looked up and down the road, like he didn't remember which street took him home.

– Go and sleep now, Matthew.

Not that I've slept myself.

Sleeping less and less, in fact, as the last few days have done nothing but prove him right over and over.

We *should* have known.

We did *not* pay enough attention.

It was arrogance, on our part, to think we'd so much as glimpsed what was happening.

That was less than a week ago, and when I woke up this morning I knew I wouldn't leave the house.

Just like that; it's begun. A stretch of days where the only task facing me is scratching out page after page as if there's some purpose to noting all of this down. Their only true purpose is the false sense of order they create, and though it's false it soothes me.

I know they are the one habit I'll keep for as long as it proves possible.

I'll know the end is close when I stop writing things down.

When I think: I'd wanted so badly for my parents to survive into old age.

If they were still here, would I tell them?

Would I go to their house and tell them that, because of the work I do, I have access to particular information, and that though I have promised not to share it with anyone, though there could be repercussions for saying what I am saying out loud, I nonetheless have to tell them? Feel obliged in my heart's core to tell them?

Such are the questions I've been spared, as an orphan.

Not that one can be an orphan at forty. I could be a widower, but that would have necessitated intimacy of an entirely different kind. A closeness I never felt especially drawn toward, but whose benefits I can see more clearly as the years go by: to have someone turn to you and say *I would feel it if anything happened to you, I would know if you died*.

Similarly, I might have been a parent whose child had died. There's no single word for such a person. No noun ascribed to a parent who has outlived their offspring. Perhaps they'll come up with one soon, out of necessity. Because children, too, will be affected. Whatever they think, now: children will be affected in sufficient number that the bereaved parents will want a name for themselves – some nominal term cobbled together from all the other kinds of grief we've come to know.

*

I'd anticipated there'd be some bristling confusion but not such gross, wilful misunderstanding. Emma kept on pressing her hands together and saying

– I just can't wrap my head around it.

And Kent

– I don't follow your logic.

The faces of these people who I have taught and trained, who look to me for guidance every day, who my instructions have lifted out of danger. I said

– If you saw a trout swimming downstream you'd know it was sick because it needs to swim upstream in order to eat and breathe. If you saw a snake trying to breathe through its mouth you'd know it was sick because its mouth is for gathering scent and scent alone. These behaviours that are inoffensive in and of themselves turn sinister in a certain context – a certain animal.

But they were confused, distracted.

– You say he was purring?

Not the first time they'd been asked to believe in something they have not seen, and yet they couldn't grasp it. Not the first time they'd been required to act on something invisible. And yet, they were resistant.

– The purring was only an initial symptom.

A glimpse of the strange behaviours he would have performed. Most likely grotesque, corrupt. Certainly: unseemly.

But no matter. It's only an addition to the tumult set to streak through the world.

No matter if they think I'm mad after all I've taught them, after all I've seen.

No matter.

I know what I know.

The mouth is an orifice that should not weep red.

Old men should not purr.

I think of Matthew knocking on the door to my office. I think of him eventually opening the door. I think of him leaning on the doorframe, saying my name like a curse.

I think of him rubbing his eyes, and saying *Goddammit, Koan.*

I think of him making his way through the tasks I've left him and watching the clock, watching the door. Hoping I'll appear, tricking himself that he sees me.

But I told him: all I can say is what I know, what the signs and symptoms divulge.

They feel compelled to question my logic: fine.

Let them find their own way.

People overcomplicate Nature because they think her driven by something crude and fallible, something akin to human logic, and so they detect false errors and instances of cruelty.

The simplest answer, the route most direct: *that's* what we must look to.

What we know: when an interior, biological shift occurs within a species it is in response to an alteration in that species' environment.

What else we know: this new environment is proving more hostile to some of us than others.

Not an extinction, then, but a purge.

Matthew

Three things happened in quick succession.

First: animals and vegetation started changing.

Second: we were given hard, clear proof of the planet's truncated lifespan.

Graphs and plans, measurements and timeframes. The most basic and tedious materials that shaped our work every day only they'd something new, now, to tell us.

Once this proof was public, people started to group together.

We'd mostly anticipated everything that would come to pass; false idolatry, mass suicide.

All of that, that particular kind of mayhem, started happening quickly and didn't catch us off guard.

We traced everything back to changes in atmosphere, temperature; of course the animals were growing more feral, more wild. Their nervous systems were being over-whelmed with as yet invisible alterations. The pigmentation we put down to a sweeping infection. Seismic shifts had seen the release of a long-dormant compound, and where it struck mammals it caused inflammation. We were alert to it but, as Koan would say, it didn't very much alter the land-scape of our concern. Not at first. Though anything marked with red was arguably more dangerous because it was now more erratic, capable of prolonged and vigorous frenzy, nothing was a predator that hadn't been one before.

Remarkable, looking back, that even at this late stage we were still forgetting ourselves as a part of nature and its rhythms.

Because the third thing, of course, was the people.

People stoked up with fast heart rates and violent hungers.

Lying down in the street.

Panting, purring, clucking, cooing.

It was difficult to string into sentences what it was you were seeing. Their inflamed parts, *that* you could put a name to. But the rest of it. At first, when we spoke about it, we mostly exchanged single words.

Swoon.

Fever.

Delirium.

Right away Koan started saying things we weren't ready to hear, was adamant these people couldn't be saved, but that was so entirely typical of Koan. I told him

– You're treating them like feral cats, these people.

But then it became clear – whatever about panting and purring, whatever about sore-looking skin.

Whatever about any of that, it was the things we saw once it went public and everyone knew we were living in an altered world. When we saw what else they wanted. What they'd already done or might do.

That was what pushed the last of us over the line.

Anna

Mother always said Koan was clever but that there was a lot he'd forgotten or maybe had never known. Why she taught me her own red lessons.

In the dark woods, kneeling beside me,

– Not all red things are sick things, bad things.

There were things that were red before, she said, and these were things Koan would never speak of. Facts and truths he kept blurry because he liked how the blurriness kept us in line. Like when you asked him a question and he said something like

You know what happens to a body when it trembles. You've seen a fox crouching with its mouth stretched wide.

She told me all this from when I was young, very young, so I wouldn't die of fright when my bleed came.

– There's red and there's red.

Once she showed me her own, put her finger inside herself and then daubed it once, twice, on the lid of each eye.

– Helps you hunt, she said, a carmine tint for your night-time eyes.

The woods humming around us when she cleaned her bloodied finger on her tongue.

– Your body won't turn on you. Don't let Koan tell you otherwise. There's plenty Koan only thinks he knows.

It hurting to turn red, for instance; maybe that was a mistake of Koan's or maybe he meant to lie.

Mother never said outright it wasn't true, just laid it out in front of me. Took me to see my first red woman when I was twelve. We'd gone very far into the woods, much further than usual. I know, now, because she was willing this exact thing to happen.

Mother said

– There, do you see her?

And I did. There was no way to miss her. Pale woman passing through the gorse – the snagging thorns, their pattern of open scratches. I thought I'd know it because the sight of her would frighten but this was how I knew: the way she moved.

– Can you hear her singing?

And I could. Throaty and lilting.

– What do you see?

Which was another way of saying *How do you know?*

– Her mouth.

– What about it?

– It's too red, much too red.

– What else?

How do you know it's the dangerous kind?

And I could see this woman was licking her lips, like she was drinking the pain of passing through the thorns. Like she wanted more of it. Either it wasn't pain anymore or it was still pain but she was liking it. Either way, she for sure wasn't *hurting*.

– What'll she do if she gets any closer?

– She'll put her ruby mouth on mine.

– Do you want a red mouth like that?

63

– No.

– Do you want your legs all scratched and bloody?

– No, Mother, no.

Remembering this red woman now it's strange that she had a body like mine. Her thighs about the same width, her breasts about the same shape. Almost like I started growing into the space she left behind once Mother shot her.

– It's normal to cry, but remember – it's a fine line.

This she said after, because I was upset. Upset at the sight of this stranger's body moving toward the ground.

– It makes you feel better at first, but before you know it all your good salted water has slipped away.

Knelt in front of me and holding my head, a thumb pressing under each eye. Catching the tears there, saying

– In five breaths' time, there'll be no sadness left.

And she was right, somehow. After five breaths the sadness had left me.

Still, I didn't want to go into the gorse and salt this woman with her too-red mouth and her stinging thighs. I wanted to lie beside my mother on the cool soft moss. But she said

– No, there's no time.

And again, she was right: there wasn't. Somehow, in this place where we're always waiting, there's never any time.

And then there were lessons I didn't know were lessons right away.

– You ever get a funny feeling about Tobias or Lucas? Or David or Matthew?

– No, not especially.

64

Where were we when she asked me this? At the shore? At the stream? Somewhere private, must've been.

– Well. Someone like Lucas, Tobias, David, Matthew – Koan, if you're near to any of them and you get a strange feeling you run. You don't have to tell them why you're running, you just run. And, if for some reason you can't run, you cut whatever part of them is closest to you. You get them bleeding, and then call out loud and don't stop calling.

None of which made sense to me, and I tried to think what made Lucas, Tobias, David, Matthew and Koan the same.

– What about Adam?

I remember now. We'd stopped at the stream because she'd felt like bathing. I remember because of how she looked at me, when I said my brother's name. Her body, outside of its clothes, soaking up all the wet dark of the water and the night.

– What if Adam makes that feeling in me?

Stepping out of the water. Gleaming black hair.

– Shouldn't happen. But if it does, the rules are the same.

Fastening her clothes around herself.

– And where should I run to? To wherever you are?

This last part she didn't answer. This was Mother's way: to decide you absolutely needed to know something, and then get tired in the middle of telling you.

It'd be a while, still, before I got to read Koan's journals and realize how little she'd told me. That she'd told me less than half, telling me how to avoid the wants of men. As if the wants of men is something I'd spend my days dwelling on. And she'd told me nothing about my own body and what I could do with it, what certain parts were made for. How the parts that felt like hot coals could also feel sweet, feel like silk.

She left that to the hawk, to show me.

The release, this evening, waking up and feeling my bleed had come.

The trail behind me on my way there, saying *Come sniff me out, tread your cloven feet across me, spread me over bramble and gorse.* Some tracks where something came trampling through the red ribbon sorrel.

Back to the shore. Even from a distance I can tell that the tide is rocking and low. They're gone. All of them. Not a sliver left behind.

Back into the woods, away from the coastal water and its moonshine. See my hawk in a tree. Watch her unfurl her wings and make them shudder.

Telling me she sees me, answering my body with her own, and looking at the huge feathery cloak of her wings I know that *Yes, there – that is the size of me.*

The size of my body, my body which is mine and mine alone.

My body which knows its name, keeps its own time.

Kneeling in the stream to let my crimson flecks drop pale in the shallow water, vermilion clouds making spatter their hot cardinal rain.

Drop after drop, carrying their message downstream.

Red Storm coming
red wind, red rain,
red hurricane

On my knees, my body listening to the creaking trees, night-time wingbeats, those creatures in the water – the feeling they made in me. In the pouchy skin of my stomach and the worn soft of my thighs, where my flesh is tender and quick to bruise, that is where I felt them.

Constant, tugging and slow.

I know I'm still marked by their slow shiver, when my hips first begin to move.

Afterwards.

As always.

Mother's voice, her finger on my eyelids.

The skin there warm with remembering.

Koan
Vol. 1
#4

Matthew came today.

I'd thought he might, because it was announced – at last – this morning.

I heard him calling, walking around the side of the house, opening the creaking gate that divides the front and back gardens. I watched him trying to see inside, stepping to and away from the kitchen window. Nothing about how he was dressed or how he was standing gave away anything about what's come to pass. I went downstairs and let him in and he said he wouldn't sit down, said he'd been sitting for days and his body was sick of the feel of it.

Matthew has always been an angry sort of person. He said

– How are you?

And what could I tell him? That I was awake all night but forced myself to stay in bed until the first hint of brightness, at which point I moved through the house and made sure all the windows were latched shut, made sure every door was closed? Not just the doors you might go outside by, but every door – bathroom, kitchen – I closed every one of them, even wedged a towel under some, and then I sat on the floor in my study which is at the back of the house.

That, still, I heard them. The loud streets and the people who were making them loud. I heard them as a din in the distance and I saw them on the television for the four minutes I could keep it on.

Instead, I said

– You walked here?

And he nodded.

– It's mostly quiet now.

I thought of the debris that people make simply by moving. He said

– And you've been all right, here? All right by yourself?

– I live alone, so it feels normal.

– You've had no trouble?

– None.

His face tightened as though this displeased him, that I haven't been tormented. No need for him to know I haven't been sleeping. That at night it seems I can hear the clouds curdling. No need to tell him I let the shower and kitchen tap run and run, wondering what's been percolating in the pipes, their metal made porous by the agitated ground. We still don't know, precisely, what caused it. Where it came from. How closely the two are tied: this sickness surfacing in certain bodies, and the planet convulsing. Shredding at its ancient seams.

– And you? No trouble where you are?

– No, it's been quiet.

Matthew always seems to get taller the longer he's standing. His spine takes a little time, but it lengthens. He rubbed a hand over his face in one swift, upward motion, said

– I keep waiting.

For it to start, he meant. The chaos we've been expecting.

69

What form it'll take at the very beginning we cannot know, but I would wager landslides. Seabed ruptures. I was picturing this, felled mountains and the oceans churned to foam, without realizing my eyes had trained themselves on Matthew's chest. The shirt he'd on hung loose at the collar. Whisper of dark hair growing on his chest, flecked with copper.

– We've been talking. The others and me. You were right.

To which I said nothing.

– Now that they've seen it for themselves. It's making sense for them.

He looked at me in that hungry way of his, but I had nothing else to share with him, there being no fresh evidence. Besides, he had told me nothing I hadn't predicted.

– I don't think they understood, before. But you were right.

And then, rubbing at his eyes,

– About the purring. About it only being the start. They've seen now that you were right.

A part of me wanted to ask what he's seen, what the others have seen, but when I opened my mouth to do so my stomach rose up inside me. I made to lick my lips but my tongue was dry. Then, he said

– I've been thinking. We should go somewhere.

By now I was sitting down and I was level with his hands which were raw from the biting damage he's done with his teeth. He said, again,

– I think we should find somewhere to go.

This: the real reason he had come.

– Somewhere to wait it out, you mean.

– It can be a bit more than waiting, but yes.

– Who, exactly? You, me and Tabatha?

– And the others. The others, now that they've seen . . .
We all want to go somewhere.

– And what do you need me for?

– You're the only one who saw it for what it was. You
always see things faster, without a filter. They forgot that,
and they're sorry for it.

Rubbing his mouth now, sad laughter gone into his
palm.

– They've turned very sorry, the last few days.

Again the question moved in me and again my stomach
clamped, queasy feeling shot into my loins: *What have they
seen?* What had happened that they could no longer ignore
what I had spelled out for them? What had happened that
they now understood what they'd called madness and mis-
interpretation when I explained it to them as simply as I
could? When I said *Think of what we saw in the broadest
possible terms: a red substance making its way out of the body.*
A distinctly feminine process. Menarche, oestrus; these are
the only plausibly healthy, the only plausibly *normal* reasons. Any other demonstration is a cause for concern.

Matthew was still talking.

– Might be fine being alone here, now. But in a month,
two months . . .

I said nothing and he knew what I was thinking: *Almost
anything is tolerable, provided it's not for ever.* So he changed
tack.

– That way you'd have control over your days for as long
as possible.

Until, until, until.

71

– I don't think so, Matthew.

– People will want to get told things, and they'll get told something. Might as well be you. Makes the most sense that it's you. Given the things you know.

Matthew thinks me a certain kind of man because he's seen me keep my head. He thinks I've a way of handling people because he's seen me corral volatile men, but these were all situations when we were out in the world, working. These were all people I'd never see again, and I controlled them because the alternative was impossible: that a family would stay in a house though a flood was coming, that we would lose an irreplaceable sample. These were all situations in which the end result was attainable, and the means of attaining it entirely clear.

Matthew doesn't know that when we first realized what was coming I went into the bathroom and screamed, let the terror bounce off the tiles.

Of course, of course, of course it was coming. It was inevitable. It had always been inevitable, but it had never seemed that 'inevitable' would pertain to our lifetime.

And today, those words on the screen. I kept waiting for them to lose some of their punch, some of their meaning. But they didn't, and ever since I've been dissecting them, rearranging them. Making them face the other way.

Diƨaƨter

Cata-lypse

Apoca-clysm

– How about I come back in two days?

– Matthew—

– You can still be saying no, you'll just be saying it in two days.

Smooth, clean table between us. I thought of my study. Thought of lying down.

– Are you thinking of somewhere in particular?

– That trip we made, last year.

He means after the call came in about a bird that flew to the same spot every morning and kept climbing and dropping, never resting or hitting the ground. One of those first embarrassed calls when the caller didn't even want to leave a name, but knew they couldn't go another day without telling someone about this strange, subtle thing they'd been losing sleep over. At first we thought maybe she'd seen hawks mating, talons entwined and rolling toward the ground. But when we got there and we saw the bird – we knew right away it was too large for its breed. Too large and entirely misshapen all over, even its beak seemed swollen.

I know we're not supposed to walk there.

That was the first thing she said, worried we'd scold her for climbing over a fence and ignoring the hazard signs. Perhaps it wasn't the first time she'd tried to report it, and it had gone badly before, because she wouldn't leave her name. Not even a nickname, which Matthew had teasingly suggested.

When we found it, the bird's nest was high up in a tree above a patch of ground, and the ground was smoking.

– To think, Matthew said, the size of that old mine.

Then he climbed up the tree and went quiet in the branches. At least ten minutes he was gone and I got so tired of waiting and calling that I kicked the trunk. When he came back down – something in his arm, against his chest: the nest. I couldn't believe it, that he'd done such a thing, but then I saw what he'd seen. There, in the centre of the tightly woven sprigs and branches, a nest not empty, but not filled with eggs. A nest that was filled with stones.

Now, in the kitchen,

– Just think on it.

– I will.

But it made me sad all over, that such a place, a place that was empty because people were afraid to carry on living there, now seemed a place that we should go. A place atop a fire that will keep on burning. A moment of thoughtlessness so thoroughly marked by flame. Whatever natural toxicity had been in the coal heightened by everything they sent gushing in, afterwards. The slurry, the ash and the clay. Pumping foam that filled up every crevice and every rivulet crease.

Poison fire that disappeared a town. If not all of the houses, the people and the postcode. All of the electrics, most of the plumbing.

– And whatever happens, you won't have to keep it up for long.

A tired sound coming out of me that might have been a laugh on another day.

– Well. That's true.

But I did not want to go. Even now I feel my heart getting larger and faster at the thought of it. I felt him watching me, waiting. I shook my head.

– No, Matthew. My God, you'd really go back there?

– If it means going out with a little composure.

That made me laugh: composure. What could be more crude than living out the last of your life over a trash fire thriving down a coal mine? I said

– I think we're past that stage.

– The dignified stage?

– Yes.

– You're probably right, but it'll be worse in the cities.

– It's the people that'll make it worse, not wide roads and tall buildings.

– Right: the people. Those sick people. We go there, no one will come near us.

– We can't know that for certain.

– Think of where it is. Think of that road.

The road leading to the houses that grows so hot a mist rises whenever it rains.

– *Think*, Koan. Who would walk down that road and burn their feet?

– You and Tabatha, apparently.

– There's houses, there, and a lot of them still have running water.

– Matthew – of all the places. It might be quiet there but the smoke – that land is sick.

– We'd only be there a few months. Six months, isn't that what we said?

– Matthew. It's poisoned.

He was looking out the window now, his face and shoulders taking on the green hue of the garden.

– We're more robust than starlings.

We'd had to find the bird, of course, and when we found it we killed it. One vial of collected fluid, some incisions – all it takes for an animal to become a specimen. The bird was, indeed, too large. But it wasn't large from some mysterious spurt. It was large because all of its organs were engorged and competing for space inside its body.

Unremarkable bird, made grotesque. Lung, stomach, gizzard. All swollen so deeply and so thoroughly *rouged*, this animal that was now busting at the seams. The left lung grown so much larger than the right accounted for its lopsided flight.

But why, *why* the stones?

For days after, it distracted me, the thought of their chilled edges meeting with her folded feet. The confused bird wondering what else she could do to keep them warm.

To think that, not so long ago, such a paltry thing had been sufficient to alarm us.

Once Matthew left I went back to my study and lay flat out on the floor, using my body to block the door. My books and my journals covering the walls in their ordered rows. What would they tell me now, if I read them? Would it sit before me clear as day? Clues that we were foolish in looking to Nature as a force that will, at whatever cost, instil and restore order.

Matthew

The night before I went to see Koan I woke up and Tabatha was sitting in a chair looking out the window. She was making a strange sound. That was what had woken me: Tabatha at the window, saying a sound which was my name. Her breath on the glass. A shirt she'd been sleeping in riding up her thighs. She'd tied her hair back but most of it had come down. I was half asleep, said

– It's freezing.

The heating was still on a summer timer, had been broken for months and we'd been putting off fixing it. The whole night the house had been cooling. Again, she said

– Matthew.

I didn't know then this would be one of the many things I'd later wish I could unsee. If I had I might've taken my time getting to the window. Whatever it was Tabatha was seeing, there was no question I'd have to see it too. But I might've lingered a little longer in the heat of the bed, looking at the back of her head, her curls bright with lamplight.

I was still a little innocent, then.

That old man purring had been strange and it had gotten under my skin, but I hadn't seen what Koan had *seen*. I'd seen a man undergo a reaction – a vicious, volatile reaction. But the rest of it . . . I'd been working with Koan a long time and had seen him predict things in a way that, even after he laid it out straight and plain, felt like magic.

Yes: the man had died in a state of pleasure a younger man might've tolerated for longer.

Yes: whatever he'd died from, he'd somehow caught it off his cat.

But what it meant for certain bodies to secrete a red fluid: no. On this we were divided.

I'd disagreed with him for maybe the first time since we started working together, carried on disagreeing with him right up until I stood at the window with my stomach brushing Tabatha's crown of gold hair. I stood behind this woman I'd known since I was a child, and watched a man in our front garden. I watched a man, or the outline of a man. I watched a man who had melted into his shadow. I watched a man who was probably the same age as me tending to a stretch of skin on his thigh. Over, over and over.

Tabatha's sleep-crushed curls. Mark on the window, where she'd wiped away her own breath.

How long had she been sitting here, probably afraid to move, afraid to make too much sound, trying to wake me?

I said

– Is the front door locked?

– It's always locked.

– But you're positive?

– Yes.

She moved forward and I thought I saw warm air rush up from between her shirt and her back, but it was my breath hitting the cold air, steaming.

– I'll go down, I said, I'll go downstairs.

– I've been down already.

– What?

– I went down to look out the window. He didn't see me. He's not, I think, seeing anything.

Where the light of the streetlamp landed on this man's skin it glowed a fierce, hysterical orange.

– But you should go down and look. Go down and see.

Should have known, should have known.

In the sitting room.

Carpet beneath me.

We should have known.

We hadn't seen all of it, weren't grasping even a fraction of it. Should have known it wouldn't stop at purring, that a man would come and sit on our lawn and make me ask what it'd feel like, touching yourself like that? What happens to you, that you feel only what you want to feel and your body is taken up with that feeling alone?

Because he wasn't feeling the cold, that much was certain, out there in the muted starlight. Wasn't feeling the ice-crisp grass or the chilled mist that came in the hours before dawn. He was only feeling his own hand on his skin: scooping. That was the word. *Scooping.*

It was not an action I had ever seen anyone perform on their own flesh. I had seen people hurt themselves, yes. But not like this. Not rhythmic, careful, slow.

But for all it being something I hadn't seen before it was reminding me of something, or *trying* to remind me of something. Like a parent teaching a child to read will say *Come now, this is a word we've seen before.*

And then he turned to me and it was those words I saw on his face.

Come, now.

I saw a thing I didn't want to see.

Open, irrevocable hunger.

A hunger that would never be sated, no matter how many times he brought to his mouth the flesh that had been his thigh.

Come, now.

Knowing what I know now, I think probably someone or something he wanted sat in his lap. I think he got very close to something he'd been denying himself a long time, and the pressure he'd felt on that part of his body he wanted to feel everywhere. That part of his body had brought him a moment of bliss, and that's why he was bringing it to his mouth. For him that part of his body was the pleasure itself and he wanted the pleasure inside him.

This is what I'd come to think, later.

But all I saw just then was a man nursing a long, slippery wound. The stretch of skimmed skin evidence of an ongoing rapture that had eroded a person. Because there was no person, now, behind the gaze. The gaze itself an invitation. His eyes saying *You don't know now but soon, soon you'll know.*

He knew the answer to a question I woke up in the middle of the night asking but managed to put away for the length of any bright, healthy day: what happens when you give in? What happens when you say enough, I've tried enough. Resisted enough. Lived long enough with this choke on my heart.

What happens when you take off the muzzle?

What happens when you take it off and you don't

care who's seen you? Don't care who knows what you've done?

Come, now, come.

Back upstairs – she was waiting for me, facing the door. We were looking at one another now and I knew she hadn't wanted to look me in the face until we'd seen the same thing. In that time since she'd been downstairs, it was two different worlds we'd been living in.

– Tomorrow, you go to see him.

We'd each seen the same thing, through the dark and the rain-dirtied glass.

– The others will fall in line, once they see. But tomorrow: you go see Koan.

We thought we needed Koan because we thought he was right.

We thought he'd been the first to see something the rest of us hadn't been able to look at, never mind make sense of. We thought there was more coming that we wouldn't understand, consequences we couldn't gauge, and we were frightened. Seems an obvious thing to say, but we were. We were terrified all the time.

Adam

Anna is standing outside with a hand on the neck of the horse. Probably until she heard me in the treeline she had her cheek on his side. She looks at me and says

– Have you named him?

– Jacob.

She shoos a stinging insect away from Jacob's brow.

– You know, I thought I might take this old horse for a ride.

Putting the skins to one side.

– If I can get back early enough this morning, before the sun gets too high, I might ride him down to the shore and back.

I ask her

– Why?

She pulls on the cord that keeps her dress closed at the waist, laces it around itself once, twice, three times.

– Why not? Because it'll feel good.

– He's too old to ride.

– You rode him through the field.

– At walking pace. You mean to make him run.

She stands up and slips her hand under the old blanket we've thrown across him. Rubs his side, moves her hand to stroke his chest where his coat is thinning.

– We'll just see how we go.

I move toward the fire. Prod at its centre.

I shouldn't let this upset me, as chances are she won't have the time. Chances are she'll come across something that's dangerous because of its hunger, or else dangerous because of its size. Something big enough to hurt us if not tonight then some other time. Maybe a red moose knelt down with its nostrils flaring, a red bear bolting upright before it starts charging.

But I can't stop thinking about it. Her body on Jacob. Their closeness.

I can't stop thinking about it while we eat and I'm yawning and Anna's eyes are flashing at every other sound.

– All right, Adam. See you in the morning.

Jacob's the first pet we've had for a time. Mostly if an animal is old enough or calm enough to stay near you that's a sign it won't last for long because anything calm or old enough to keep near you is likely to be easy prey – trusting and slow. When we were younger I'd a doll and Mother thought that was perfect; a quiet thing that kept me company but couldn't go red, wouldn't die. For years I thought it had blood on the inside. A little heart and a little stomach and a little tongue in its shut mouth. Eventually Anna told me no, the doll was hollow, and then she knocked on its stomach knowing I couldn't deny the sound. When she put the doll back in my lap it looked ugly to me and I broke it as soon as I was alone. This thing I'd been sleeping with and holding at my side. It was a lie. And so I broke it. Broke open its face and chest with a stone. Sure enough: empty.

I threw it in the fire but it only melted and stuck to the

wood, all the while making a thick smoke that made me spit and spit while it burned.

When Anna saw what I'd done she said

– She was just being a doll.

Like I said, we'd a strange way of learning things. Everyone was always trying to explain something to us, but still a lot got confused or lost along the way.

In any case – I like Jacob.

His bad ears are a match for my bad sight.

And even if we didn't have something in common, he keeps me company all through the daytime.

Every morning now, once Anna has gone to bed, Jacob and I come to the stream together and while he's tethered to a tree he drinks from the water I'm lying in. There's a part of the stream where the water runs just right, where I can lie down and feel the streambed beneath me and the water running over me. This part of the stream that runs thinly enough that any intrusion at all, say the moving mouth of a thirsty horse, is enough to flood me until I feel the air inside my lungs, panging.

Sometimes I can tell by the sound of his tongue in his mouth that he's wanting water, but I'll just wait and wait and then wait a little longer, just to be certain that when we get to the stream he'll want to lose his whole snout in the stream where it runs shallow. His frenzied thirst making his snout plunge deep so the water runs high and hard over my open mouth, fills me quick and sets my chest bucking.

When I sit up again: my heart on fire.

Jacob still there, his gentle face dripping.

I wonder how much salt I might put in his food before he stops eating it. I wonder if I could take the rope that loops his neck and pull him down, down. I wonder what feeling it would make in me to watch his broad neck bending, to watch him drink past the point of thirst. I think I would do it: put that sore feeling in his throat to feel the stream jolt in my own.

Too often, I know, I asked Anna to go over the night Mother left. Asked her over and over though I knew she'd tell me the same thing: that they'd gone out together and parted ways at the usual place, and then Mother must've looped back, gathered up some of her things, stained the floorboards, left again.

But then, every so often, there'll be a glimmer of something new. She'll say something she's never said before, like she knew something had happened as soon as she came in the door, but it took her a little while to realize what, exactly, she knew. Telling me that she must have been in a daze, coming up the stairs to wake me, because she walked right over the stain. Didn't see it until she was in the bed beside me.

I remember waking up and seeing her there. New lines around her eyes. A new hardness to her mouth. These things telling me maybe not that Mother was gone, but that something was broken, and that from now on we'd be living inside of something that wasn't meant to have happened.

– I think Mother might have gone away.

– And isn't coming back.

She nodded, lying on her side. Some small tough leaves caught in her braid.

Black flame dancing right up my centre. Sooty, smoky heat. The way she nodded, I felt it in my own neck, her every gesture I felt in my own skin. Our limbs tugging toward one

85

another. Not just sibling closeness but a pair of bodies for-
cibly uncoupled, waiting to realign. Anna saying

– We have everything we need.

Squatting beside the stain which was not yet dry.

– Everything will be fine.

A lie told in love is still a lie.

The blushing shadow the stain left on the soles of her
feet. The stain that was Mother loving us. The part of her
that loved us had fallen out of her, and made a mark on the
floor while it died. Anna pulling a rug on top of it, telling me
to stand on it, saying we couldn't give up a thing to Koan.

Koan always worked to keep his feelings tucked away
but when Mother left they came up in welts and blisters.
Raw patches of skin dotting his lips and the insides of his
mouth. He was red hot with it. I remember thinking his
heart must have been sizzling, there in his chest.

Anna went to tell him and she came back with him
steering her by the shoulders – it was just after morning
worship and so everyone was still outside and they saw the
two of them like that, Koan with his too-tight hands on my
sister. Heart thrumming while I stood on the stain and
thrumming harder again when he sent us downstairs and
we had to keep calm under the sound of him moving around
the bedroom.

The room where our quiet bodies spent time sleeping.

Me, Anna, Mother.

I looked at Anna for as long as it took Koan's grip to
leave her shoulders, the pinkish marks fading slow.

There were others who came by the cottage while he
moved around, searching for Mother like she was a wilful
child hiding away in a cupboard, but who were they?

Annabelle, Jeffrey, Florette? All these names with no faces. Whoever it was they waited until Koan had come downstairs and gone back outside before it started: Where'd she gone? How'd we know she'd *left* and wasn't *missing*?

Koan just said

– She took her winter shawl.

Meaning, as it was only spring, she intended on being gone for some time.

That night was the first night all my dreams were spent looking out from behind Anna's eyes, seeing things my own eyes couldn't see – moonlight hitting the coarse edges to the long grass, the blue-black pebbles that line the bottom of the stream.

And the next day, like any other morning, I went downstairs to stoke up the fire.

And, like any other morning, when Anna came back we talked a little, made worship.

But with her neck in my hand I made my own private devotion:

Strong sister, precious twin.
Streambed partner, cut away kin.

– Shake our hearts, Storm, with Your thunder, only come, Storm, come.

Anna

Slow sun today, taking its time in rising and setting and so my knees feel torn with the drawn-out devotion. Down to where the grass turns crisp with the sea and then further to where the wolves sometimes do their savaging, the soil there reddy with little cubs' bleeding. The wolves will die out if they're not careful, killing off their young. But then all they're doing is all any of us can do, which is the thing that makes sense at the time.

Tonight when I wake I know I've dreamt of Mother. Tight anger up and down my body that I tell myself is the work of forgiving.

Though, the older I get – the anger less at her for leaving and more at myself for staying.

That morning: salting and salting the soles of my feet where I'd stepped in Mother's red, knowing this salt was taking away the touch of my mother. I was cleaning my mother off my body. My mother had become these marks on my feet and I was scrubbing her away. Flecks of blood, by the time I was through. But that's what you must do, when red has touched you.

I inherited her eyes and I inherited her heart, so some of what she saw and felt I know in my own body. The rocks along the shore, gone all slippery with moonshine and the shine a pull on your eye – the shine a call to you, a promise of pleasure in the water. Feeling of being a bowl of broth someone wants to eat before licking clean the spoon they ate you with. Thinking *If I'm to be eaten best make sure I'm scalding hot, best make sure their tongues are blistering.*

Those first nights without her I kept wondering how long it would take me, running a straight line into the woods, to find her. Let myself pretend she didn't turn red. Pretended I could track her like a deer and come upon her with her hair down her back, knelt beside some animal and using her two hands to keep its gutted belly open.

How like Mother it'd be, to have carried on living with her red heart or her red eyes or her red throat, just a little further away than our usual stretches of ground. How like her it'd be to lift her face and say

– You only needed to *look* for me.

Because we never did, not really.

I'd have followed her that first evening if I could have seen how Adam would be all these years later.

Would have caught up with her and said

No, there's something you have to fix before you go.

No woman ever did so little to receive such blind devotion.

Impossible to have a mother and not love her, I know. Impossible to have a mother and not let your eyes run blind over her flaws. But Adam nurses a mother I'm not sure I ever met – shelters this mirror version of her with his sick vision. The mother he aches for doesn't have coarse palms and a hot tongue, wasn't equal parts devout and blasphemous, ill and strong.

The woman he misses is not a woman who would have left us anyway, eventually.

Not a woman who, red or no red, would have eventually found a reason to go.

I know it was seeded in her, that she would leave us, and I'm afraid if I think on it long enough I'll know it, too. Her brutal logic. I'm afraid I'll hear it and I'll leave Adam here to wait on Storm and do his best with Koan.

And so I don't think of her.

I will not think of her, and what she did and didn't know.

Still.

Sometimes when I wake it's with my whole flesh singing because I dreamt the nuts and bolts of leaving, and my heart and my arms and legs all think I'm ready to go. Once: I almost managed it.

I kissed him one time. Clumsily and through the hair on the back of his neck because he was sleeping on his stomach with his face pressed into the sheets, and so I couldn't reach his mouth. Not until I was out of the cottage and down the path did I say, out loud, Goodbye, brother, and even at that distance I thought my voice would waken him. Thought everything he'd ever said about seeing through my eyes might be true. Shiver of shame through me now, to say it – that I didn't walk, I ran. Ran from my constant sibling, his wounded heart and weeping eye. The feeling of running was the feeling of drinking the clearest, most quenching water. The feeling of putting distance between us. I ran and ran and every animal, every tree was

Mother, waiting. I thought *This must've been what it felt like when she was leaving.* She must have felt her whole body singing and everything, every new quick wound along the soles of her feet was part of the song. When I stopped, this was why. Because of course the shadow of her pleasure had been our grief, a shadow neither of us would have survived without the other.

I looked at the moon and she seemed different to me – instead of her profile, her chin's underside. I realized I'd never come all this way up the track, there being no need as it only leads, after miles and miles, to the steaming road. Never before had my brother and I been this far apart, and I could see the loose threads of our apartness behind me on the ground. Cold, silvery threads that I looped around my wrist as I made my way home. Not running, now. Walking though it felt like crawling. Like pressing my shins through stone. Every step the feeling of Adam's hungry lips, hungry eye. Back at the cottage I'd no stomach to spend the rest of the night in the woods, just sat with my back against the kitchen door and said something I'd never let myself say before. I said it knowing I would only say it this one single time.

– Come home, Mother. Please come home.

When Adam came down in the morning he saw the grey smudges 'round my eyes, the lines 'round my mouth which deepen whenever I'm tired.

– So it *was* a strange night.

And I played along, said

– How did you know?

– I'd the oddest dream. It went on and on. Strange trees, strange moon.

– Was it frightening?

– No . . . not especially. Mostly sad. From start to finish; sad all over.

Koan
Vol. 2
#26

When I saw her coming down the path I thought *A wolf has learned to walk on its hind legs.*

Even now, hours later, my body is sore with the terror of those few moments – that's all it takes, when the terror is pure and absolute, for havoc to streak through a body. Muscles spasming, jaw clamping, believing I was seeing a hybrid wolf.

But it wasn't a wolf.

It was a woman.

A woman who must have lived a previous life as the broad-muscled leader of some matriarchal herd. A woman with an old injury around her hip which was dictating her gait, causing her to lope in this angular way.

A woman whose ghost-white skin drank all the light so it seemed she was covered with a glowing pelt – the soft fur running down an animal's underside.

Remarkable, that at first no one else noticed her. There, in the clearing in front of my house where we build fires and boil water, everyone was involved in some kind of labour and didn't turn at the sound of her footsteps. It had not occurred to them that this might be someone new, a strange face to see. And she, in turn, didn't look at anyone else. She walked straight toward me, more and more of her body coming into view. Dark, dark hair. Sinewy shoulders, a splash of freckles around her collar. A mouth winged with the lines of an older, more sun-damaged woman. Beneath her eyes: veins, electric blue. I cannot remember the colour of the eyes themselves, only the unnatural pigment beneath them. A few feet away from me, she opened her mouth to speak and I thought *What will the words sound like, coming off her wolf tongue?*

She didn't tell me hello, didn't say her name.

All she said was

– Matthew told me I should come.

Another treachery from Matthew, another indiscretion. But I put that to one side because, by now, I could see her stomach.

She had on a shirt and the shirt was riding up on the taut, round flesh. Just one of the buttonholes puckering, but it was enough. I could see. Flash of skin that was a little leathery with being pulled too smooth.

– How far along are you?

– Why?

The word came out of her so quick it seemed we'd spoken together.

– If Matthew told you to come he must have told you some of the questions I'd be asking.

She made no move to touch her stomach in any of the standard, protective ways.

– A little over two months.

Two months, and the size of her.

Twins.

– You're of course welcome to stay if Matthew knows

94

you and can speak to your character. Has he told you how we live here?

Litters in other mammals, yes, *those* I've had the opportunity to analyse.

– Yes.

It seemed to me the pregnancy wanted to take up more space in her body but she was refusing it passage – that was why she seemed to hum at her edges: she was using some inner mechanism to keep it contained. But: twins. She would have to yield. Two bodies, suckling. Yes. She would have to yield eventually.

– Has he told you what will happen when you give birth?

She moved one hand, now, around to the base of her back and began to knead the muscle there. The motion of her wrist pulled up her shirt and I saw it: a wedge of scar at her iliac crest. An old trauma still thrumming, panging with every step. It might give her some trouble in labour.

– I don't follow.

– There's a room we use. You'll go in there and I'll come with you, to make sure.

– But I'm having twins.

– Yes, I can see that.

– Matthew said it would be different with twins.

– And he was quite right, the risks are less. But there are risks all the same.

I understood that Matthew hadn't told her this before because, if she'd known, she wouldn't have come.

– No.

Which means it was a risk he didn't want to take.

– I understand your concern, but it's all very respectful. And a necessary precaution.

– No.

Why? What about this woman made him adamant she should come here and live with us for the time remaining?

– Well, then. You're free to find somewhere more suited to your needs.

– There is nowhere else, and I've come a long way.

– I've told you what must happen if you stay. That's all that's required of you, save your share of labour, and on that front we take into account your condition—

– I can work just fine.

Matthew stepped out of the treeline. It seemed he'd already been working; probably clearing the path between the cottages and the stream. His sleeves were rolled up, his cheeks flaming. He looked at this woman and said

– Eula.

I don't know if she was happy to see him. She did move, slightly – very, very slightly – toward him. But her face stayed the same and she said

– This man is saying something about watching me give birth.

His shirt was sticking to his chest, the skin there sopping wet. It's still winter but the air is close, here. Your clothes feel clammy once you start moving, working.

– There's a lot Koan knows.

– So you said, but I don't see why he needs to come into some room with me while I'm in labour.

Matthew looked over his shoulder, probably for Tabatha, but whether because he was hoping she would arrive or hoping she'd stay away I couldn't say.

– He sees things the rest of us can't, figures things out faster.

– That's all well and good, but I won't have a stranger with me when I—

– In seven months I won't be a stranger.

She looked at me and I felt it again: shiver when you realize yourself much too close to an animal.

– I suppose I'm wondering what makes you special.

An agitated sound from Matthew. It's a habit of his; nervous barking laughter. He rubbed the back of his hand across his mouth and into the callused skin across his knuckles he said, again,

– Eula.

– I'm asking because I'm curious. All I see is a man who likes telling people what to do – who likes telling *women* what to do, which isn't exactly uncommon.

As she'd been speaking, the others had noticed – started listening. Matthew said

– The things Koan knows, the things he's figured out, they've kept us safe.

Some of them were leaning against the trees and others were on their knees, but they were watching us. She was our first stranger. The first example I'd have to set.

– If you're not comfortable with how we live here you can go have your twins in the woods and watch them get eaten by a wolf.

She turned to me with her face alone; her body – her stomach with its prize – she kept directed at Matthew. In the veins beneath her eyes, a flickering. Before she could speak again, I said

– It would be a frightening thing, I think, to give birth

alone. Enough to drive any woman mad, the sound of her children crying when you don't know who's listening, who might follow the sound.

Across her chest – her shirt was moving. Her heart was pounding hard, now. That had done it: the thought of her newborns crying in the silent dark of the woods.

– I wish you the best of luck, finding somewhere. I do.

She looked to Matthew, who said nothing.

– But if you want to stay here, there's rules we all follow.

Her lips came open, slowly. Just open enough that I could see the off-white tips of her teeth.

– You like to frighten people. You're trying to frighten me.

– If you've any sense you'll have been frightened a long time.

Laughing, flashing me her palm. The sound of her laughter; anyone who hadn't been looking at this new woman was looking now.

– I keep my fear here, in my right hand. Any time the fear gets too much I remind myself I can just cut my hand away.

Her lips back together then, streak of pink with a peach outline where the wind had worn some of the softer skin away. Laughing one more time and then, to Matthew – *not to me, but to Matthew* –

– I'll stay.

The blood coming back into Matthew's cheeks like his nerves had been keeping the flush at bay. I said

– So you agree, then?

– I said I'll stay.

– Everyone who lives here lives by the same rules.

– I hear you. I said I'll stay.

She said she'd always lived alone and wanted to be somewhere as quiet as possible, so she's in the cottage furthest from mine, from all the others. The one whose bedroom has a view of the bay.

When Matthew and I were alone again I said

– Who is that woman? How do you know her?

– I met her about a year ago.

– I don't know where to start. What does Tabatha think of her?

– Give it time. You'll be happy she came.

– What did you tell her that's made her so suspicious of me?

– 'S just the way she is.

– Overly cautious?

– Alert. And didn't you see?

– See what?

– That bag she's carrying. She has a gun.

– A gun?

– A shotgun.

I wanted to ask him how, why? I wanted to tell him the thought of this coarse stranger with a weapon slung across her shoulder wasn't exactly soothing to me, but I could tell by his tone he was getting ready to feign distraction and wander away. Although Matthew never really wanders, he's simply adept at hiding his purpose. He turned from me and the light caught the dark hair that runs down his neck. Lit it up with an auburn tinge, smouldering fire.

– Matthew, I said, don't do that again.

And he nodded, a quiet settling over the half of his face I could see.

– Couldn't even if I wanted to.

Meaning there is no one else, or at least not any way of reaching them. The world turned to a bank of sand, and every so often another shelf falls down.

The things I would do, were it not for Matthew's background lingering.

I imagine, for myself, an ancient translation of his name: *Matthew, a wound no one notices until it's weeping.*

Lately, it seems he likes the feeling it makes in him, to resist and question me: tight swivel of power.

It gives me no comfort to remind myself he's not an evil man because there's no such thing as evil, only an ability to discount the trials of others more effectively. No comfort to remind myself I've known him a long time, that Tabatha has lived with him for years. Probably Tabatha has her own reasons for letting things slide.

But still: twins. *Twins.*

Impossible to predict what they'll tell us. Impossible to overestimate what they'll confirm or reveal.

No: there's no denying that this was, all things considered, a very good day.

Anna

Of course, as I'd spent the morning thinking of Mother, this morning when I opened Koan's journal the first line I saw was a line about her. I was looking for something about the see-through creatures on the shore but instead my thick thoughts called this page to me. He was barely awake in the chair and I could have read and read in the quiet but no, I let the damp pages come closed.

Our mother was a fault-rich woman but Koan always took too much pleasure in running through her vices. He saw her going as the first stage of his sparkle waning so that, later, he was too dull, too blunt and faded to stop the others leaving.

Only way he could comfort himself: to take her apart with his pen the way he never could with his tongue because he was frightened of her. Frightened of what she'd turn around and say.

All these old thoughts rocking around inside me from half glimpsing one line. I don't even have to see her name to know it's her he's writing of –

I thought motherhood would soften her.

All he ever wanted from any of us. To be *soft*, meaning agreeable, meaning silent.

Back at the cottage; Adam's hand a cold choke while we made devotion.

When I came on to the stones he was already waiting there, kneeling with his arm out, his cupped hand ready for me.

I want to keep him calm, keep him happy, and so once more I knelt beside him, once more bit my tongue and stopped myself asking why he thinks we never once saw Koan on his knees.

And then dusk came down like a curtain, another night starting.

The moon is only a sliver, at first, but quickly she gets larger, turning 'round. Her bright, pockmarked body felling its shine while I dry off in the grass.

Mother once let slip that when she was a girl she was never let out alone in moonlight, and then she asked me

– You ever miss the sun?

And I told her the truth, which was

– No, not especially.

Tonight, when I went to the shore – wingbeats in the trees.

Small ones.

The sound of something else, inside the tree. The wood swelling and breathing.

Those animals really are gone.

Up to my knees in the surf, looking. Proving to myself they've left.

Or else, waiting.

Could be they'll come back.

Could be they've something else to tell me.

Adam

Mother's leaving mattered most, but it wasn't the first.

David left a note behind, saying he couldn't wait on Storm even one more day, that he was worn out with waiting. Colette left because she had a red baby and lost sight of Storm, Her grand logic and Her high purpose.

Whenever we asked Mother where they'd gone she'd say
– Not so far away.

But Anna said David had eaten a poisoned flower after he'd written his note and that she'd found Colette strung up in a tree. She said they did what Storm would have done for them if only they'd waited, and because they couldn't wait they died sore and brutal.

The last person to leave before Mother was Elena-Vaye and that was different because she didn't want to go. One day Koan came and found us, told us someone was leaving and we were to come and say goodbye, and then he walked us up toward the farrow room and Elena-Vaye was standing there, scuffing her feet over and over in the dirt of the track that turns into a path and then a road.

Anna said
– Why is she leaving? I don't understand why she's leaving.

Mother was there, and the others. Not all of them, but most. Mother looking at Elena-Vaye from a certain distance away and that was how I knew, how the both of us knew. That careful distance we all knew by heart: no less than twice the length of your own body.

When the red man comes and you feel his carmine tremor,
times two from the tip of your head to your littlest toe,
that's the keep-safe measure.

– The children have come to say goodbye.
But Elena-Vaye didn't so much as look at us.
– No need, as I'm not leaving.
– You'll only prolong your own suffering.
– You're caught up in your dreams, Koan.
– If you don't leave of your own accord—
– And now you're threatening me like I'm some stranger.
Someone else asking her
– How long have you known?
Behind us, Koan's hands on our shoulders. Pressing us forward, just slightly forward, leaning down and whispering
– Just a half-step, just enough to feel it.
And we did, we felt it.
– Known what?
Spit rising up off my tongue like the field births water when the stream has flooded.
A tender ache in my pelvis. Even now, when I think of her, that's what I feel – right away, that ache comes back to me.
Mother putting two fingers to her bottom lip, saying only
– Elena.

Because Elena-Vaye's lips had started to pulse ruby before us. Elena-Vaye who bent deepest for Storm and was never not kneeling first thing at night, first thing in the morning.

Carnal, carnal woman.

Red through and through.

I can't remember her face, I remember none of their faces, but I remember her mouth. How she kept dabbing at her lips to keep the redness down but it kept replenishing, kept wettening though she kept dabbing and dabbing and then furiously rubbing. Her whole sleeve sodden.

Koan:

– Do you see?

Slippery tremor. Taking up too much space in my body. Anna had put a hand over her low stomach: a flat, braced palm as if she was afraid her body was about to let slip her child's womb.

Koan, again,

– Can you feel it?

Mother looking over to us and saying

– That's enough, they know.

Turning back to Elena-Vaye,

– You should've said. I'd've packed for you.

I tried to take a step back but Koan's body was there behind me. I thought I'd burst with it, the quickening.

But then Elena-Vaye herself was taking a few steps back and away, not troubling any longer to wipe her mouth. Sanguine stream trickling down her chin, her dark throat.

Telling Koan with this mouth that was no longer a mouth, but a wound – a wound which was the point at which she'd weakened,

105

– Don't send anyone after me.

He might have nodded, there behind us. He might have nodded because he meant it, or just to see her on her way.

Afterwards, for days and days, I couldn't be alone. Couldn't sleep for the fear that Elena-Vaye would come back and lay her body on mine. That she'd hover with her gushing mouth above me, dripping red and red and red.

Within a few weeks, Koan was weaving her into our lessons.

– You remember her: a woman so red that even saying her name put you in danger. The syllables of her name enough to sew red seeds on your tongue. And what do red seeds turn into?

– Red flowers.

– Imagine: red flowers growing in your belly, all because you'd swallowed some red seeds off your tongue.

Elena-Vaye. She taught me how to skin a rabbit. Once helped me out of a tree I shouldn't have climbed.

Never again did we say her name out loud.

Anna

Watching the clouds shadow the sea. A coarse look to the rocking foam. A few times I let myself believe those animals have come back, but mostly I count the waves as they curl up to the shore. An old habit Mother insisted on: look for the highest wave, the only wave that, if you looked away at just the right time, would carry on rising.

Sitting by a whale bone and thinking about the night they washed up here, how we heard them before we got to the water. Heard them as soon as the wind died down and stopped making crackle the trees.

Everyone moving toward the woods, moving toward the sound.

Stepping one by one out from the treeline.

Later Koan said it couldn't be true, not once they were out of the water, but we'd all heard it, the sound they made: mournful, wistful.

– What are they called, Anna?

And I'd said

– Soft-Coo-Mountain.

Because they did seem, just then, like mountains. I'd never seen a thing so large. At that time hadn't seen anything come out of the water.

Mother nodded, said

– Whale.

And then,

– Something must be happening pretty deep in the ocean.

But at least a few of us, in those very first moments, thought it was the beginning of Storm. Elena-Vaye went down on her knees in the surf and started making devotion. She put her closed fists right into the beachy ground and stayed on her knees 'til someone pulled her up again. When nothing happened, the others started to catch such and such a smell, such and such a sound. Headed back into the woods.

Turning back on her heel Mother told me I mustn't touch them.

– Could they be red?

– No, but it would be cruel, bothering them when they can't move.

But I did. Once she'd left, I touched one of them. Put my ear against it. Whispered

– Loud fish.

My mouth on its stomach,

– Tremendous slice of ocean.

The sounds coming from their giant slack mouths were nothing like the sound coming from inside them, which was the sound of a wall coming down.

Not until the first hint of dawn would I see they'd eyes and venous openings to breathe through. I'd thought all they had was a mouth and even their mouths were not mouth-shaped, were open slices. I waited with them too long, wanting to see as much as I could – then had to run hard so as not to miss devotion.

I didn't know they'd soon be a line of moist bones and that Mother would be gone.

I didn't know I'd soon see my hawk, and think my red

had come because I felt all the things we'd been told to look out for: a tremble in the heart, the muscles 'cross the hips rising. Didn't know I'd make myself swallow the terror and say *If it's happened, it's happened.* But the night moved on, and no red came though I carried on feeling the heat and the slippery feeling this bird was bringing me.

Although Mother had told me about Koan, shown me a red woman, shown me my own body, I don't know if I'd really understood, through and through. Until she was gone. Until I saw my hawk. I don't know if I understood that a lot of the time when Koan was speaking he was also lying.

Koan
Vol. 2
#89

Today, when I first saw Oliver weeping, I misread his face. I thought *Someone who's been eating and sleeping alongside him has taken a blade to his smile.*

But no. Not a knife.

He was screaming because he'd gone walking and found a bobcat eating its kitten, had come across them just in time to see the mother use her tongue to fold the baby's little nub tail into her mouth. I told him the kitten must have been sick, that a mother knows best for its brood and that it can be a kindness to do such a thing. A terrible kindness. But he'd gotten close enough to see how the lids had worn off the mother's eyes to leave ruby orbs behind and he couldn't stomach the thought that this was how we would go. Eaten alive, eaten slowly.

A man I'd hired as soon as he'd graduated and had never so much as shaken his hand. A grown man in my lap and my body twitching at the closeness, at all the things you can see in another man's face. How the lines around his eyes lessened when I told him the worst of it had already come, and that the final moments would be unknowable: a matter-of-fact obliteration, an immediate consumption.

I could feel all the others at my back now because I was

saying things I hadn't said before. I said to him *It's coming, it's coming* and every time he calmed a little more and it was something I'd never seen, words cooling down a person. An effect as quick and efficient as a glass of water, as being given a blanket after too long in the cold, so I said *Don't worry it's coming soon* and he said *Tell me again* and I said *It's coming, I promise you it's coming* and he asked how I knew and I told him how every evening I could see an increasing discolouration in the skyline, how the soil was threaded with an electric-bright root. I told him that every morning I went to look at the sea and each time I went it was saltier, that if he went there now he'd see it: sharp crust of saline that would crack like glass under his foot.

What I didn't say out loud: *I can feel it. That's how I know. I can feel it coming.*

I've been feeling it since I first saw red seeping out of a grown man's body. Behind the purring: another, second vibration. So deep as to be almost silent; announcing itself.

You were waiting for me, and now I will come. Am coming.

But what I did say out loud he took into himself like a tonic.

It was just like Matthew had said: *All people want is to have their hurting lessened. You just tell them something simple they can hold on to. Doesn't have to be sparkling or new.*

And then, Eula. Seizing on a moment when she knew I was distracted. In front of everyone, she said she's been hot since it started.

Since 'all this' started.

Simple as that.

I should've known she was working to keep something hidden.

111

Always more flushed than she should be and I thought it was the weight and strain of her high round stomach but it's because of this – her constant, even fever.

I asked her to go on but she wouldn't elaborate. All she said was the one sentence over and over: the last few months she's been pestered with an unrelenting, all-over heat and now it seemed to be settling so that she could manage, with certain tricks, to keep herself cool.

I kept looking at that hard hill of a stomach, thinking how much more difficult that would make sending her away. Because no matter how banal a change it is, it's still a change that's been working its way through her – in a month or a week, who knows what she'll be. For all we know it's a first sign of her red starting, a sign we haven't yet seen, and any day we'll all be weeping and staining. Leaving tomato-red smears on our seats.

I hoped Matthew might say something but, as is his way, he'd caught scent that something difficult was about to happen and had wandered off, feigning busy.

We haven't spoken much since she arrived, and it seemed strange to be saying her name, telling her to leave.

But she just kept on looking at me, and then the others started talking. In a chorus they told me how at least ten of them had felt these small, unremarkable changes; hotter than they'd ever been, needing hardly any sleep. Changes they hadn't thought to comment on, thinking them an off-shoot of panic, their bodies finding new ways to keep them moving.

I listened to them one by one, but all the while wondered how much of this Matthew already knew. I have tried, since, not to distract myself with what else he hasn't thought to tell me. It's always his habit to hold things back, here and there, if it's likely to save him a confrontation. But that won't do here – he should know that. It simply will not do.

This morning, down the slight hill from the house where I've been sleeping, into the nest of cottages, I thought she was standing in a smothered fire. I thought to myself *That's how hot her blood is, that she can stand in these hot ashes and not bat an eye.* But when I got close enough to hear her tapping her tongue on the roof of her mouth – right at the front, right on that bulbous mound – I saw she was standing in the dewy grass and the warmth of her had set it steaming.

I understood, without asking, that she'd been asleep and had grown heated between the sheets.

I knew, without her telling me, that this was something she did every day, and today was simply the first time I'd seen it.

She looked at me – or rather she glanced over her shoulder, and I happened to be standing in the right place to catch her eye.

– Morning.

– Morning.

Turning just enough to her side so I could see the ripening peach of her belly. Not for the first time, a tremor of gratitude that I was born the way I am, with a body like mine.

– And what'll you do with yourself today, Eula?

– Find a way to keep cool, mostly.

Meaning to rub her hot blood in my face.

– Even a little bit of sun sets me flushing, now. I'd sleep all day, if I could. Swap all my days for night.

Tabatha

The trees.

Three of them thick-trunked, the other two still-slender saplings.

Which one is she?

I can guess by the width and the height but I don't know for certain. It was something I made sure I never knew. Even Matthew thought it would be a comfort to me but I said

– No, don't tell me. Never tell me.

But I think I'll know when I touch the bark.

I'll feel all the lost touch at once, because I never touched her.

Not even when she was born. Not with my hands.

I wonder if there's anything that'll trickle out my palm and through the roots, wonder if there's anything at all I can—

Adam

A woman is coming toward the cottages, cutting through the crying trees. One after another she puts her hand on the trunks as if a soft touch is all they need to stop mewling. Ahead of me Anna is squatting in the long grass, watching.

With every step she is closer to us and with every step I think *Please, please.*

She has on a sort of tunic that drags and catches behind her, and the way she walks gives me a tugging, over-the-shoulder feeling, something stepping in and out of my good eye.

The half-light keeps shining pale and she's yet to look at us fully so she keeps getting closer and closer and still we cannot tell.

Behind us a cloud shifts and a fraction more light shines through. If Anna does shoot this woman we'll have to wait 'til after devotion, to salt her. Cleanse ourselves in the understairs room.

Anna is bouncing a little now like she means to take off running. Her mouth will be full of a prayer to Storm that this woman will just be a woman and not a red woman who means to make us lie down in the grass and do things we'd never otherwise do. But I cannot bring myself to pray. I only keep thinking *Please, Storm, please.*

Only a few more moments before Anna breaks with the

waiting. She's said it before, that the cruellest part is not the shooting but the waiting.

The maybe-red woman has stopped with her back to us, her hand firm on one of the oldest trees.

What if she tricks us into touching her? What if her breasts are her red parts and she tries to give us rusted milk from her teat?

And then, quickly, Anna stands up, clearing the grass and hooting – high, animal sound. The woman looks to her right away – she shows us her face. Her eyes, swept with carmine. Red veil her face has been living behind.

I can't help it.

From the back of my throat: bleating sound. I dip down into the grass so that anyone watching might think the bullet passed through me and this red woman at the same time.

Anna's mouth; I imagine myself inside it alongside that hopeful, useless prayer. Warm crescent of her side; I am pressed against it. There is no safer place than my sister. Her body which is its own climate, its own skyline.

My sister who is calling to me, and when I stand up I see her pointing at the sky.

The both of us running, Anna's steps falling soft and rising high.

Storm has to see your crown, yours has to be a body with which She is familiar.

We run through the cottages and on to the stones, kneeling fast and hard, knees stinging through their calluses. Our hands on one another's necks, each weighing the other's head down, showing Storm our crowns.

– Come, Storm, we are ready. We are ready, Storm, come.

*

Before the salt, before Koan, we go back to the dead red woman.

I say

– Looks like it started in her eyes.

So thick and so strong, down the sides of her face and thickening under her nose so that her mouth could be any shape. I turn to keep watch of the road when Anna starts to salt her, putting them in line with my bad sight. After a moment there's a pause in the rush of it leaving the bucket.

– Anna?

– Nothing. It's nothing.

Then Anna drags her away, back through the trees, which are crying hard. The sound of them follows me back to the house where I rest my face alongside Jacob's and feel the gentle scratch of him against my closed eyes.

– You're so lucky, Jacob, you don't hear them cry.

And he feels the hum in my jaw while I'm talking and breathes out, loudly, which is his way of making a reply.

Anna comes back and she's tired, after digging the hole. Too tired to talk or even look at me.

Anna

Something about that woman.

I had to hurry to dig the hole because the sun had risen, but when I put her in the ground I squatted and spent some time looking at her body, her face. Her chest, where the bullet went – right under her left shoulder. The blood orange of the wound a perfect match for the caul that started 'round her eyes and grew to cover most of her face.

How did she live with it? Her vision must have been crissed and crossed. Her nose and her mouth – everything she smelled and tasted.

The red woman won't rest 'til you've swooned at her side.

Things Koan said those days he could feel our attention slipping, when we weren't the right mix of attentive and frightened.

– Do you know where the word *crimson* comes from?

I said nothing but felt Adam move beside me, the tussle of his head shaking.

– There used to be a red worm that lived in a small, evergreen tree. It was so small and stayed so still, people thought it was part of the tree. They thought the worms were seeds the tree itself had made. They took the worms, which they thought were seeds, and ground them for a red dye, a dye which they called crimson.

Looking from one of us to the other.

– It was only later they realized the little red bodies were living. That they were worms, not seeds.

Still looking. Adam's white shoulders beside me.

This was before I'd seen his journals. Before I saw those cramped sheets where he'd written our lessons over and over, tweaking them 'til they were tight and impenetrable, a fist wrapped 'round a bone.

– The root of the word *worm* is *cruim*, do you see?

In the very corner of my eye: Adam's mouth dropping open, coming closed.

– And *cruim* became *crimson*.

The both of us, by now, were nodding. Koan looking over our heads, reading in the clouds how the weather would unfold.

– It was the pregnant females that turned red. The pigment came from the foetuses. So small they couldn't be seen, and yet they changed the colour of their mother's body.

Wanting only to be away, now.

– Those husked bodies that were turned to dust.

Wanting to have grown up in some other place, to have been born on some other day.

– They were punished for their redness, their deception.

Adam's shoulder, his arm. Our skin where it grazed, buzzing.

I was making a promise to the both of us, inside my head. I was promising that *Soon we'll be running to the stream. We'll have our feet in the cool water.*

– It's very important you understand: there was always something suspect about red, something unbecoming.

But who knows why this woman has me thinking about Koan's worms clung to an evergreen tree. Probably because

119

it was the pregnant worms that were battered and pounded, and this woman moved so slowly through the trees where the red newborns were buried and their mothers, stripped of motherhood, afterwards moved like they'd been beaten. One trunk after another she pressed her palm against, like she could hear the crying Adam always talks about. Like they were having some effect on her. But then maybe she was just feeling her way because of how her red had grown, blurring her sight.

When I do dream it's of Mother's bloodied finger, my lids crinkling under its quick pressure.

Koan
Vol. 3
#10

– What happened to you, Koan?

She caught me off guard, coming up from the stream. I go early in the morning so as to avoid the others and it has become an unlikely pleasure: stepping out into the dawn, walking into the bracing water to bathe.

– Eula. Good morning. Trouble sleeping?

– I've been watching you and I think I've just about cracked it.

– I see.

I hadn't bothered to dry myself off. I'd planned on walking straight back to the house as usual, and putting my body in front of the stove. Even a few moments with Eula; enough to put a chill in me.

– One thing I know just by looking: a man who doesn't like women.

– You've too much time on your hands.

I thought I'd taken a half-step around her, but looking down I saw I hadn't moved.

– You're always in a knot about what makes for a good mother.

– Everyone else spends their days cleaning, cooking—

– I think your own mother must have been quite the woman, one way or another.

I couldn't help but laugh. Even though my cold feet were panging, now. Even though I was shivering.

– My mother was not a woman—

But here my tongue seemed to slide down my throat, just slightly and just enough to choke me. I tried to swallow around it, speak again.

– My mother was not a woman who—

And again: the sentence ended of its own accord. My cheeks turned to cotton, my breath hurting and shallow. All the more maddening: Eula's placid gaze. She didn't make any move to comfort or alleviate me; though my face must have been flushing she showed no concern. Just watched me and waited, waited. It seemed we stood there looking at one another for so long the light had time to change and we were no longer in the very earliest, simplest part of the morning.

But my vision had just dimmed with being dizzy.

I chose another sentence.

– She wore her wounds lightly.

– And had she many?

– Many what?

– Wounds, Koan. Had your mother many wounds?

The one time Eula wasn't painfully, infuriatingly literal. She thought I was referring to some sort of psychological grievance, where in fact I was referring to a very real, very physical sore in the flesh of my mother's thigh. I remember seeing it for the first time and the sound of her voice when she told me she'd been bitten, bitten by a dog named Ralph. Ralph was an impossibly large Dalmatian, and I think she meant to put some charm in the wound – to turn it into a palatable story. Everyone in the neighbourhood, after all, was well accustomed to the sight of Ralph bounding down the street. The younger children often made to grab his tail and no one stopped them, no matter he'd been known to snap.

No, my mother couldn't have known how my child mind would twist and bend around the terror that a dog's saliva had taken root in her leg. How I came to believe that the sore marked the development of a large black spot of the kind that appears in a Dalmatian's fur. At night I would creep down the hall and stand outside their bedroom, my eyes adjusting, making certain it was still my mother in the bed and not a damp-nosed canine.

The smell wafting out of the room on those warm nights: lavender-scented powder she used to keep the wound dry. The quilt itched her and so she'd sleep on her back with her leg out. The window open. Her nightdress catching in the wind.

She'd never have thought I'd have been less disturbed by the simple fact of a venous ulcer, and indeed she never told me the truth of her sickness – never uttered a word. I had to uncover it myself. Years later, by sheer fluke, I came across an image in a textbook and thought *Who took this photo of my mother?*

None of this, of course, I said to Eula. To that woman, who doesn't know the meaning of the word *hurt*, the word *wound*, I said

– Only one, but it needed constant tending.

– Well, there must have been someone else.

– You know, I'm sure Tabatha would appreciate some help with the saplings.

– I'm not saying you've never had a good reason to dislike a woman, but one woman for sure got under your skin.

– You don't know me the way you think you do.

– But I do know you, Koan. I do. I've met you plenty of
times before – in other countries, other towns. Different
hair, different colour eyes. But it was you.

– Let me alone, now, Eula.

– I'd know you anywhere.

– Are your days so empty that you've nowhere else to be?

Laughing, the laughter moving her shoulders and her
throat. Her mouth didn't move, and I was glad. It's a fear-
some sight, Eula smiling.

And now, though I am so tired I would shorten my life by
a whole day if only it meant I could sleep, I cannot shut my
eyes. Cannot stop thinking of Eula and the pleasure it gave
her to drink up the sight of me floundering. Cannot stop
thinking of those hot nights, staring in at Mother. Waiting
for her to take shape in the dark so I could put my fear away
and sleep. More than once a wind rushed through the open
window and her nightdress flared up: a silk tent above the
whole of her soft, pale leg. The dark creases where the long
white muscle met with the rest of her body. Caught in the
strong winds that mark any summer storm.

Those nights when I began to understand the female
body in its fullest, ripest form. Distended fig, swollen
pomegranate. Fit to rupture with its thousand seeds.

Adam

Anna goes to bed and I feel her sleep pulling on me, weighing my eyes closed.

Three slow days since the woman in the trees, and I worry today will be another day when the hours come treacling and everything takes longer than it should.

The traps. The clay.

To help pass the time I sing, a little, which I cannot do when Anna is here because she hates all of our songs.

> *I saw a red bird and it had a red nest so I shot it with my*
> > *gun,*
> *I saw a red woman and she was breathing loud from her*
> *red red red red lung.*

– Adam?

He appears just as I'm shrinking my nose against a too-strong smell off the sea. Such a tall man and on his forearms and neck a crust of foam.

His limbs are strong but his mouth is chapped and his eyes are pink, made sore from the salted water. When he parts his lips to speak I see their corners have been made tender, have been made split. The exposed flesh shines like the inside of wetter fruits. Again, he says

– Adam?

And I have to accept it isn't some nonsense sound he's making.

– It is you. Adam.

It is, in fact, my name this man is saying.

– Adam, don't look so frightened – I know you didn't forget me.

Koan
Vol. 105
#28

I happened to be at the right spot to see them coming out of the trees. Matthew and Eula and Eula's daughter. Something about the way they were walking, the distance they all kept from one another. The child sulking, refusing to make worship. Trying to go straight to their cottage, saying she'd go get her brother. Eula gathering the back of her shirt into her hand to keep her in place.

I said to Matthew

– Where were you?

– Only down at the shore.

Eula moving the child away and saying something to her, her voice very low.

– Did something happen?

Matthew letting out a long breath.

– Eula showed her something she maybe wasn't ready to see.

– And why were you there?

Looking back to me now, which meant he had to look down.

– What's that?

– What was your role in this moment between mother and daughter?

– I know my place, I do what I'm told.

– The child seems pretty shaken.

– Take it up with Eula, 's her daughter.

I could see it, Eula and Matthew lying down together with the girl only a few feet away.

– You'd want to be careful.

He was looking around for Tabatha now.

– You're getting carried away again, Koan.

When did he start speaking this way to me? There must have been a moment it shifted, but I missed it; was looking the other way. Was being *obliged* to look the other way, at someone's needs, some communal concern. And while I was doing that Matthew was forgetting that I am the one who saw Her coming, I am the one who has always known. The one who saw from a thousand miles away what red would do to us. He's forgotten and the forgetting let him stand there mocking me like it cost him nothing.

The boy came out of the cottage, rubbing his eyes in the morning, going to kneel beside his mother less than ten feet away. Eula between her children, her long arms and the bend in them – they looked like wings robbed of their flesh and feathers, white as bone. A child underneath each hand, and them reaching up to hold on to her neck in turn, their fingers interlacing.

Matthew already gone back to Tabatha, who takes his body in her hand like it's nothing. Does she feel even the slightest risk, when they're touching? Does she ever stop and think about what such a man, such a body can do to another person?

Another way that red has proven dangerous: wherever it is absent, we presume ourselves safe. But just because a person's red isn't showing, that doesn't mean they can be trusted.

It certainly does not mean they're good.

part ii

Spoor

Adam

Looking around him and his clothes twist with moisture. The trousers he is quick to take off and my chair is the closest thing to drape them over. Inside the wide collar of his shirt I see salty crystals glisten at the base of his throat. When he sits down and his knees come up high I can see that all over his body his hair is thick with it, that every strand is thickly covered with the glittering salt.

– Any chance of a drink?

I turn around to pick up the bucket, full and cool with the stream's clear water. Too late, I realize I've turned my back on him which we are most certainly not supposed to do. But he shows no sign of it, no sign at all. Behind the salt: bright and healthy skin. His breathing and his way of speaking – everything seems normal. Standing with the bucket's sore weight on my hip and he's looking at me as openly as though I were a tree, something living but incapable of returning glances. I look at him hard, look him all over while I kneel down and put the bucket on the ground. He laughs, says

– Look all you like, nothing to see.

I dip the cup into the water and hold it out to him. From here I can see his stomach, its hard muscles, his polished-looking sex in its nest of salted hair. Only red thing about him is a tint, at certain angles, to the hair at his temples.

He takes the cup in his hand, his hand which would fit around my head, and the touch comes as a shock to me. He looks at my face, looks at the cup. His legs are so long that his thigh is a low wall between us. He takes my fingers in his hand and pushes them against his lips, moving them around the curve of his flaking mouth where the skin has come away from itself in small, dry feathers.

His eyes are so alive with sting and blood I don't right away notice they're green.

I put my fingers in the water and now he opens his mouth and tilts his chin toward me. His tongue is leathery, white and blistered at its sides. I move to take my hand away and he takes hold of my arm, suddenly strong, and starts to move his tongue around my fingers as if they'll give up more water. I move the cup closer to his face and pour the water straight into his mouth. He gulps and drinks but keeps my fingers there, inside himself, the slow motion he makes with his tongue sending the water down the sides of his face and a squirming, cruel tingle through me. His hand is too tight on my wrist, pushing back the thin hair so that the skin starts to itch and ache.

My hand is an animal, there in his mouth.

Trapped, edible.

We're close enough that I can see the freckles 'round his eyes. I can see the other colours that make up his hair. I can see the dark wet hollow of his throat.

I see more of him than I mean to see.

Enough to see there's no red which is precisely what he's showing me, making me look inside his body.

I look away instead – look into the trees. And when they give up nothing, at the sky.

Today's clouds are wispy and thin.

If they drifted any lower they'd snag on the pine's branches.

Look down the sloping hill, toward the sea: the triangles the waves make in pitching forward.

I can count the waves until Anna has come, which will be any moment.

Any moment she will come downstairs and I will not be alone with this man who now takes my fingers out of his mouth but still holds them tight in his hand.

– How have you been?

It seems his lips will start to bleed if he keeps talking. How long was he in the water?

– Where's Anna?

A tremor starting in me. A queasy feeling in my knees. He says

– You don't remember me.

– No, I say, I do.

Because I do, his touch has sparked me. I remember his touch and the size of his hands, the knowledge my whole head would fit snug in his palm. That shivering knowledge is something I've felt before.

Anna is here. She hasn't been awake long, hasn't buttoned her dress, and the sweat she made in her sleep is shining on her chest. He drops my hand when he sees her and stands up. He is two, three heads taller than me. He says her name in a familiar way, the sound of it caught on his breath.

– Why are you here?

– Your brother was just checking me over.

– Why are you back?

He looks over her shoulder, into the cottage.

133

– Where's Koan?

Looking around her as though he suspects Koan is in the kitchen, not noticing that Anna is angry and the anger is settling all around us.

He sits down again, lets his mask slip a little; he thought she'd be happy to see him, thought she'd run to him.

– Where are the others?

Her tug on me is firm, today. I open my mouth because hers is open; hot waxy feeling down my throat. In the winnows of his ears I can see where the cured skin has started bleeding. The tiredness on him, something you could bite into.

– I know you have questions.

Hard laugh come out of Anna's nose.

I can see now that his green eyes are hotly flecked with shards of amber. Quietly, he says

– Why don't we eat something? We can sit down together and talk.

Every time he speaks his voice makes a deeper twinge in me.

– You want us to feed you?

His name is taking shape in my mouth.

– Or we can just sit together while the two of you eat.

Anna picks up the shawl hanging over her seat.

– Do you remember my name?

I pass her a bowl and now she puts some rabbit in her mouth. Starts chewing. Says, around the meat,

– Matthew.

– Yes.

I pass Matthew a bowl and he takes it.

Anna says

– Well, Matthew, where have you been?

Looking around him as though he hasn't heard her, spoon to lips, pausing.

– How's it been around here, since us leaving?

– Been fine.

– That right.

– Much the same.

Laughing to himself.

– You can always come home, isn't that what they say?

The spoon disappears inside him, comes back out again.

Anna finished her small meal already, but holding the spoon tight. I know what the whole of her face is doing though I can only see its one side. She says

– And where is it you're coming home from?

Dipping his spoon in the broth again.

– You've grown into your mother, no wasting time.

I think he says this to hurt us or to make us weak with remembering, and it works, a little – I see it catch in her face. But she keeps going, says

– Tell me where you've been.

Chewing more than he needs to on the tough little morsel.

– Koan didn't tell you?

– How would Koan know?

– But you know why we left? He told you why we left?

– Wherever you've been it's made you fond of questions.

Another soft, throaty laugh and I worry he'll say something else about Mother.

– 'S just I'd hate to bore you, telling you things you already know.

That hawk lands in a nearby tree and the weight of her perch sets it creaking.

Anna looks at the big sleek bird and while her face stays hard her shoulders soften.

– So it's been the three of you here, all this time—?

– No. You first.

– When we left—

– Never mind leaving. Why are you back and where have you been?

It strains him to do it, but he stills his face.

– We thought we might go back where we came from, but we ended up going further into the country.

Matthew strokes his bowl hard on its sides with his broad thumbs and Anna puts hers down, carelessly, so that it rocks an inch or so away. She says

– How have you been living?

– We've been living just fine. Much like we lived here.

– And you didn't lose anyone?

No red, she means. No panting mouths, no cruel desires.

He foregoes the spoon, brings the bowl to his lips and lets the broth fill his mouth. This time the bump is large when he swallows.

– Like I say. We've done just fine.

– Then why come back?

– Because we shouldn't have left you. Shouldn't have left you alone.

– We've not been alone.

– Course you haven't . . . and where is Koan?

She didn't mean Koan. She meant we've each had the other. But she doesn't correct him. Says only

– In his house. Same as always.

Sun disappearing. Shadow snagged on her face just so. Anna says

– Go talk to him.

– I will.

– Though he's not so sharp these days.

Matthew's pulse showing a little stronger now.

– How d'you mean?

– Headsick.

– He's not that old.

– Guess you could say he got old before his time.

Matthew doesn't move. Keeps looking at her close, steady.

– He'll be happy you're back, I'm sure. Go on and talk to him.

She looks at me and I start dishing Koan's supper into her empty bowl.

– Maybe tomorrow.

– Why not now?

– I'm tired. Took me a time to get here.

– You'll have to find somewhere to sleep.

– I'll set up in my old cottage.

He stands and Anna moves around him, picks up her gun. I didn't even know it was resting there, and now I know she had her eye on it the whole time.

The sun has dipped fully now and the only parts of them I can make out are those within range of the glow off the fire, but of course they can see each other clearly, their eyes having slipped into night-time. Anna's shoulders, up and down. Slow, slow breathing.

He says

– It wasn't right, that we left you behind.

I can feel the breath held taut in his throat and I'm sure he'll say something else but no, he's leaving; we listen to the sound of him lift his half-dry clothes, his feet on the

stones. I'm about to whisper Anna a question but she's lifting me by the elbow, pushing me inside the house.

– Lock the door.

The wood thick between us, but I hear her still.

– Lock it, let me hear you lock it.

And I do, I turn the key. On the other side she puts her
hand flat and firm against the wood and I do the same; hit
the door with my palm one time. I leave my hand there,
listening. One, two steps – then nothing. Gone to feed
Koan, gone to hunt and spy on Matthew.

Matthew.

Tall man come out of the sea.

It's too much – another person moving and talking in
their particular way. Another person with their own habits, their own turns of phrase, with blemished cheeks and a
wavering hairline.

Up the stairs and into bed, feeling trapped by even the
light sheath of the blanket, I try to remember. Did he ever
help me build a fire or, seeing that I'd cut myself, wrap his
hand around mine? I play for myself the way he moved,
wait to feel some spark in me. Do I remember the way he
looked kneeling on the stones?

The sound I make, when I call out. Not a word – a gasp,
the air turned coarse in my throat, and all of me rigid.

Devotion.

The day is ended and we let it pass.

At the window – too late.

The moon already high.

Imagine a wave that always roars upwards and only upwards.
A wave that is as high as it is wide.
That just keeps going, stretching out the flesh of the sea.

Anna

Following me into the woods like I'm an old bear, lumbering and deaf.

– I hear you, Matthew.

Stepping out of the trees, showing me his outline.

His shoulders a dark block of shadow, weighed down by his hands which are heavy with being strong. More than his voice, his hands are familiar to me. I'd been walking straight toward the shore. No way I'd lead him to the hawk or let him see me in the stream. I don't care what habits he kept with Mother.

– Plenty more woods for you to wander through.

– Maybe we can talk a little.

– Right now I don't have the time.

A laugh that isn't a laugh, a laugh that's anger.

– I swear I could be talking to your mother—

– You must really miss her, you want to talk about her all the time.

– Don't you?

– Not especially.

– It hurts, I know. Being left alone.

– Not hurt I feel so much as tired.

And then I bite my tongue seeing how his whole body settles with pleasure, because I've admitted to something out loud.

– So what, you think you can set things right by following me around in the dark?

– We need to talk a little.

– Said I don't have the time.

– We've already waited too long.

– We haven't been waiting on you, if that's what you're
thinking.

– That's another thing – Adam.

– Don't talk about my brother.

– He's sick.

– We're all sick. What does it matter? This close to Storm.

Some quiet which is the sound of him thinking, plotting.

– You know things he doesn't know.

Koan's journals with their crinkling pages.

He couldn't know – he does not know.

– Come again?

– Almost like you've seen something you weren't supposed to. Whatever it is, since we left – you've gotten out
from under Koan.

What would happen if he knew I'd read them?

– You're pretending.

Not like he can punish me. Still: flutter in my throat.
He'd have glimpsed inside my head.

But no, he doesn't know, says

– Or maybe you've both seen something you shouldn't
have. One saw something and was ruined, the other saw
something and was saved.

– Sounds like you have it all figured out.

– Whatever happened you got to keep your own
thoughts. You know the difference between a circle and a
straight line.

– You think Adam can't tell one shape from another?

– You know what I mean.

– I don't.

– You know a line is something you climb over, and a circle is something you're stuck inside.

– You sound like Koan.

– Well, he'd plenty of time to rub off on me.

– Been a while since you've seen him.

But I know a hundred years wouldn't be long enough to shake Koan off your tongue. The rhythm and lilt of his speaking. It wedges in the ear.

Now Matthew leans more on the other foot and I can tell he isn't done.

– Have you noticed anything lately? Milder heat in the summer, even in the daytime?

– I've no use for sunshine.

– You've noticed nothing? No changes?

– This is why you came back? To talk like this?

– Just wondering if anything's struck you as curious, strange.

– Most things, most days.

– So you know by now – Koan wasn't always strictly truthful?

Turning away from him. Will do me no good, him knowing the things I know.

– I know you saw Tabatha.

I'm ready to say it, *Who's Tabatha*, but I can see her. Soon as he says her name.

Up and down, his shoulders broad and high, and looking at him I can see the outline of a woman beside him. Fair, willowy. Careful. Mother's sometime friend, Matthew's pair.

– We haven't.

– She came back looking for you.

Feeling her way through the trees. Veil thick enough to hide her face.

– Well, she didn't make it.

– Not possible.

– We haven't seen her.

– She was coming for you and she knew the way.

– So why was *she* coming back?

And why didn't they come back together?

– I'll trade you.

I move the strap of my gun on my shoulder, mostly to remind him I have it.

– Tell me that you saw her and I'll tell you why she was coming.

– She didn't come by here, Matthew.

Our voices rising, the two of us a bright pocket of noise in the dark.

– Tell me what happened to her and I'll tell you something you'll want to know.

The smug way he says it, like they didn't change anything by leaving. Like I'll play along with him after he left me here with a sick brother and an old man I can't stand the sight of.

– You know, I think it was you who was always seeing things you weren't supposed to.

Some things I remember clearly, others only in part – stones I can throw, and maybe one or two will strike him.

– You've not grown up properly, being here alone. You've grown right into the mould Koan made for you.

– Adam doesn't remember, but I remember.

143

His nervous tic of rolling his shoulders. I can see them now: tight, slow circles in the dark.

– I'm sure there's plenty you think you remember.

In the hours before dawn, at the shore. At the stream.

Me.

Matthew.

Mother.

– I remember my mother thought you were a dog.

Now, he takes a step.

– She talked about you when you weren't around and those were the words she used – *barking, muzzle.*

He takes another step and takes my arm in his hand. Pulling away, wasting a bullet into the ground. Spurt of earth between us.

Loud, ugly sound. But it works; he moves away from me.

– I know you were taught to be careful—

– Don't talk to me about my mother and don't go snooping 'round my brother.

Shifting his weight, readying to walk away.

– Your mother made a mistake with you.

– Go lie down in your old wreck of a cottage, go talk to Koan.

– She hammered you like a sheet of iron, thinking she was saving you.

I bite my tongue because I want him to go, and he does – he's leaving. But he can't help himself.

– You remember it was me taught you how to shoot that thing?

Holding the breath high up in my throat: and he's gone.

I should feel some relief but I don't: he thinks he can

144

come back here and take up space again. Act like Koan with his back room stocked full of secrets.

I should've shot him for that alone. His smug tone.

Why didn't I shoot him?

Things'll likely only be worse for the two of us knowing I could have, but didn't.

Later, giving Koan his morning meal:

– Guess who's here.

His eyes shut and his face went hard all over, because of course his first thought was Mother.

– Matthew, I said, Matthew's come to see you.

And though his face softened the eyes stayed closed.

– He's come alone.

Koan even less likely than Adam to be of any help to me, but still my head is loud with all the things I wish I could ask him.

What's his real reason for coming back?

Why is he here alone?

What about the others – are they already on their way? Why send *Matthew* ahead of them?

Matthew with his glances, his habit of leaning against trees so long and so still you'd just start going about your business around him.

Matthew brought out something in Mother.

She looked at us different when she'd been with him, when he was around.

He reminded her of someone, she once said. Occurred to me then that Mother might have had a brother, but now I think it was just something she said because the time she spent with Matthew wasn't something she wanted to explain.

The mornings the three of us would walk back together, me and Matthew and Mother. The nights the two of them showed me how to kill this or that animal, how to swim in the thrashing surf.

I remember all the time we spent together but that's something he'll never make me say.

Even though Mother trusted him, nothing was ever quite right when you were near Matthew. Whether he was a sign of something gone wrong or the cause itself – that I don't know. But nothing was ever quite right.

No time to see my hawk, tonight, no time to kneel in the stream and feel the woods around me.

I have to keep circling back, checking. Each time I come back to his cottage I come a different way, and the fourth time I come down the overgrown path that winds around the back of Koan's house. There I see some smoke I wish I could unsee, because it's coming from the farrow room. Cruel, stinking room that my brother and I have no use for.

My nose pinches against the smell before I'm even close. Chilled morning light colouring its white walls a pale blue. Years since it was last used but the meat smell still lingering. These few hot bursts coming through the soil and grass is all it takes for the stink to rise up again.

The room remembering what passed inside it; involuntary spasm, wet convulsion.

Whatever else a birthing body might be, it's a body made to cramp and tremble.

Typical that Matthew would come back at the same

time the fire moves here. It set something loose in a person, going into that cottage. That room. And Matthew was setting things loose all the time. Though Matthew never went in with any of the mothers. That was only Koan. Koan was even in there with Mother, and whenever he was really in the humour to upset her he'd mention our birth. He tried to hold it over her, that for a few minutes it had been the two of them alone in a room, that he'd heard her waters breaking. He said our birth left a bad taste in his mouth, and when I asked Mother about it she laughed, said *He thought I'd need his help getting into the bed.*

I understood, though. Koan had thought he'd fashion a debt. He thought by the time they came out of the cottage Mother would owe him. He thought he'd handle Mother the way he handled those other women who came back to the cottages weepy and slow, someone waiting to help them pass the milk no one would be drinking and taking the milk away. Where did that milk go? Probably we drank it but didn't know what it was we were drinking.

This room is the only thing that frightens me. When I was younger and I came by here my hips would spasm and my legs would shiver. Even now I feel it: these walls want me to kneel, to get down on all fours and start pushing.

I keep on tracing smoke to red gashes in the ground while my tongue swells up in my mouth, trying to push away the metal taste that's coming out of the floor and its corners. Those creases lined with blood and everything else that cushions a baby. Around the back to track one last, tall plume and through the door I see without wanting to the long bedframe, the cupboard they kept full with clean cloths and towels. After the others left Adam started

147

giving me a new cloth whenever my bleed came, and it took me a time to ask where they'd come from – those very white, very soft strips of linen.

Koan said he had to oversee the births because the parents couldn't be trusted to do the right thing if the baby was born alone with maroon fingertips or a burgundy scalp. But I think he just liked being close to the mother. The smells they made. The sounds. The way they were walking when they came out again.

He said a grieving mother released a particular scent and that it was one she'd never stop producing.

– Same with any warm animal. They all have a sorrowful gland, and other animals pick up on the smell.

– What's the point though?

– The point to what?

Annoyed that I was asking a question, but one of the rare times he was in the humour to answer.

– An animal knowing another animal has had its heart broken.

– The usual reasons. Survival. Evolution. Within any species, it helps to know who's weak and who's strong.

To be sure, there's a scent off Matthew.

Something forlorn, broken.

By the time I get home again, too much sun already in the sky and he's there, appearing just in time.

Straight on to our knees, the ache setting in again.

No matter the dusk, no matter the dawn.

The ache is just the same.

Something else I don't know – what toll this'll take on Adam. Could be it's a good thing, a last distraction that'll

tide us over 'til Storm. But still, I'd rather any other creature come near me. A red bear, a swelled-up wolf. I'd take
any other creature.

Any other creature, you can guess at their logic.

Any other creature, after enough time, will give itself
away.

Matthew

The second baby was the reason we left. Would have been the reason we came back, if we hadn't seen the jellyfish.

Even now I don't know how we let it happen. Another baby. Like the loss of the first one hadn't near killed her. All I can say is it was easy to forget, while we were all here together, what your body could do. Sometimes it seemed the body itself had forgotten. How the water you put in your mouth moves to hydrate your heart. How to sleep in the darkness behind your own eyelids. It didn't seem possible that Tabatha's flesh would recall this old knowledge: how to make another body grow.

It had seemed inevitable, before, that any new bodies coming into the world would quickly be taken out of it. Not only inevitable – it had made sense. The world was dying; we were dying along with it.

We could both remember that feeling of raw and unavoidable consequence and how it had shaped us. But that feeling had left us, now.

In its place: a soft, suggestive wound.

When Tabatha told me there was another baby coming I knew what else she was telling me before she managed to say it. That it was a hurt she could not live again. A risk she would rather take.

Once we'd made the decision and no walls came crashing

down, once we remembered there were in fact other decisions to be made, it all came back again. Fresh confusion, fresh horror, fresh sorrow.

Not counting the years that came before, it didn't take long for things to click once Beth was born.

Didn't take long for Tabatha to start looking at me in her careful way.

All she said, when she eventually said it, as though reminding me she took milk in her tea,

– We left Eula's children.

And I heard myself saying

– Eula left her own children.

For months: a version of this back and forth, on and off.

But it did no good. She said since giving birth again she felt she was standing at a window and on the other side of the window was Eula. Said she could see Eula and what she was seeing was driving her mad. Said she was afraid to put Beth to her breast because the guilt had turned her milk rancid.

The only way she'd sleep, the only way she'd drink water: if I listened to her sketch out how we'd go back to them – she'd talk about 'going back to fetch the twins' with our own child suckling on her. Forcing me to think of them as what they surely weren't now but at one time had been: soft-limbed children. Day by day she wore me down, turned what had been impossible and out of the question into something certain.

She'd been drip-feeding me the nuts and bolts.

How long it would take.

Which way we'd each go.

How we'd take two different tracks, to be sure Beth had at least one parent.

We decided this even though it's been a long time since the woods and coastal roads held any real danger.

– Probably there was never any danger to begin with.

Things we could say since we'd gotten out of the circle, gotten out of the lie.

– Nothing out there that can harm us.

And then: the jellyfish.

– Matthew, if ever there was a sign.

Being back here, it smells just the same.

I told her it would and she laughed at me.

– I bet you anything, all the good parts will have fallen away, and the awful parts will be even worse or just the same.

And sure enough, soon as I came within a mile of this place I could smell it. Like I'd never left. Soaked deep in my clothes, sunk deep in my lungs.

– See! What I tell you?

I started speaking to her out loud six days ago, which is when I knew for sure that she had died.

I'd woken up in the middle of the day with my old, bad thoughts upon me and I knew she'd been taken out of the world. Like the chemicals they used to put in food or the varnish that gave wood a lasting shine, she'd been the only thing keeping me wholesome for a very long time. I don't know what kind of person I'd be if we hadn't met when we were children, and I told her so every day. She'd laugh and sigh her way around it, but it was true. Proved true once more as I lay there, watching dusk come and putting off all the things I knew I had to do.

Go look at Beth, see if her face had changed. See if some part of her also knew.

Go and talk to Elena-Vaye.

Tell her I was following Tabatha. That I'd be back in a few days.

Tell her to take care of our baby.

Three days after we saw the jellyfish: she found us.

And when she found us, all I could think was *We were wrong*.

Not a sign of recovery, of the planet realigning.

It was Eula those beached jellyfish had heralded.

Deep inside the water they'd felt the tug of Eula's stride, the orbit of her bad hip. They were like the rest of us; they thought they were acting on their own instincts but they were only moving around in her aftermath, her shadow.

She didn't speak to the others, didn't so much as glance at Elena-Vaye, who might have been the only one happy to see her. Walked straight at Tabatha and I could see Tabatha looking around for somewhere to put the baby down; she thought that was what she wanted, to snatch the baby out of her hands. Started talking at her in the same old way and Tabatha tried to convince her that she'd been planning to leave. That once she saw the jellyfish she wanted to leave, to go back to them. It had been her own decision. She just had to wait until the baby was older, just a little older. Of course, all that did was make Eula laugh. Laugh so hard her shawl came off her shoulder and I could see where she'd been stung.

Even though she had to sit down in the middle of talking, even though she was moving at half her old pace – still Eula.

Eula and her venom, her revenge we'd never stopped fearing.

Saying to Tabatha

– You go and I'll follow you.

And we were right, to fear it.

Already: an eye for an eye.

Another child who'll have to grow into its suffering.

My child – its mother taken away.

Adam

He's here when I come back from the stream with Jacob, rocking on my feet with the pang in my low gut, rush of bruises between my mouth and my belly.

He's stoked up the fire and is looking at the door that leads into the cottage, the floor with its mossy tiles, looking toward the sea and the torn-up ground.

I loop Jacob to a tree and sit across from him. He doesn't look at me, says

– I suppose it couldn't be helped.

He doesn't say the word *damage* but this is what he means. The ruin caused by years and years of weather. Endless variations of wind and rain and sunshine.

– Does Koan know how bad it's gotten?

– No. 'Spose he doesn't.

– How long has he been in there? How long since he last came out?

I'm not used to talking right after the stream. The words are loose in my throat, pebbles moving around, each of them a thing Anna wouldn't want me to say.

– I think . . . almost a full . . .

– A full what? A full year?

I can see the blood changing colour in his cheeks and neck.

– So, after we left . . . right after? That's when he got sick?

155

My head dipping; slow, heavy bell. Nodding.

Matthew worries his lower lip with his tongue, breathes in such a way it sounds like something inside him is tearing. He sits forward, with the fingers of one hand rubs both his eyes.

– And how's that year been?

His voice has changed.

– Same as always.

– Really?

– I mean. It was quieter.

– So same as always, but quieter. And that's it? No other difference?

My bad sight itching. I cover it with my hand, which sometimes helps the scratchy feeling fade.

– Yes.

More tearing; the daytime air tunnelling through his body.

– I knew Koan, from before.

I look at my knees – their rough flesh still holds the criss-cross pattern of the stones.

– We worked together. Do you know what that means? Not like the work we did here. Not separate work for night and day.

My eye paining me like he's punctured its very centre with the tip of a well-kept blade.

– I have things to do now.

I stand up, move around things that don't need moving.

– I think that's enough for today.

A nonsense thing to say, and he laughs a little at the way I say it because without meaning to I've mimicked Koan, but he gets up and leaves all the same.

The marks his feet leave in the ground.

A cloud coming through the trees.

Thick, buoyant and solitary, so that for a moment my heart leaps thinking it's Storm. Storm's smoke, Her first plume. Here, at last: the fruits of prayer, devotion.

These false starts happen so often and yet I never see them for what they are: tricks and errors and confusions. In those few moments a current has moved through me, left me ragged.

Mother's hand on me while I leaned into her hip. The waves a long way beneath us, pitching forward.

Mother saying *Look at the waves* and using her fist to knead the lump between my shoulders.

Try not to wait so hard, so long. You'll make yourself sick with waiting.

Anna's right, this old cottage stinks.

I hate the smell and I hate to think what it saw of Mother, what it keeps of her in its moist floor. What it knows about her that we don't know; whether she closes her eyes when she's hurting, if sudden pain makes her brace feet against the floor.

My arms pounding from mixing clay and carrying it, bucket after bucket, up through the cottages and down the overgrown track. My hands stained a brown they'll wear for days. Pouring the clay, watching it course down and smother each new tunnel the fire has made. Walking around the slack-jawed walls, leaning against them to ease the squeeze in my lower back.

I try to keep my thoughts on the hot ground, the clay, making sure I mix it thick enough that it chokes the flame – too watery and it just boils away.

157

But I can't help it, I see Mother.

Mother stood out in the winter and the heat coming off her so strong there was a puddle where she was standing. Meltwater which had a few moments ago been snow. Standing on a particular spot she favoured because she could see a clear path over the hills, through the trees and down to the sea. Koan once said Mother had razors for pupils and when I asked him what he meant he said *Because if she wants to see something then that's what she'll see.*

I sometimes wonder if there's a razor in my good eye, though all I ever see that isn't there is Mother.

In bed, through the window: sound of Anna coming back from Koan. She's still worked up from being near the farrow room. I hear her tossing his empty bowl down by the fire and I know she'll be rolling her neck, her shoulders. Shaking loose the feel of being close to the room, to Koan. Next she'll go to the stream and run the water around her mouth, gurgling and spitting the iron-tang of the farrow room away.

But no, another sound: she's tutting to Jacob, there on the patio – I hear her making soft-soft mutters. She wants to ride him. She means to soothe herself by putting that old deaf animal between her thighs. I cover my ears against the swish of her leg coming over his side.

It's dark but the moon is high and falling a bright hard silver, so she can take him through the field and toward the crying trees as fast as she likes without too much fear that he'll stumble.

Kneading the folds of my ear so that I hear blood, my own blood coursing, but still it comes loud and clattering.

The fall of his hooves as the two of them set out, untethered.

Her braid thumping against her spine.

Bristle of his snout, his nostrils dark and wet and open.

I'll never sleep for the noise they're making.

You'll feel better by the time the wave has reached the shore, there'll have been a change inside you.

Matthew

I don't need any confessions from Anna.

I know what happened. Feel the outline in my gut.

When Tabatha was leaving, she kept saying

– Whatever happens will be the thing that I deserve.

As if it was her fault alone that we left them and not a decision we all made together. Even then I didn't tell her what I'd seen, the truest side of Koan that I'd walked in on. Didn't tell her even though it might've brought her some relief to know that I was more to blame.

A last secret I kept for him and maybe this is what I deserve for keeping it. To have her taken from me by a brother and sister I left here to stew into people who could do that, who could kill a person.

I wonder how far she got before they shot her – if she saw them. A part of me hopes she didn't, because I know what she'd have thought. She'd have looked at those scarred legs, that sick eye, and thought *I did that*. Which means shame would have been her last feeling.

– Eula had me pegged as a better woman.

I told her if there's a price to be paid she'd already paid it. Told her penance was that first baby that came out of her and went straight into the ground.

Besides. In the end we were all pegged for better versions of what we turned out to be. We weren't meant to be here this long. There shouldn't have been all this time, too much time, and inside of it everything turning sour. That's all it is, this mess I've come back to. Rot that shouldn't have had time to fester.

It was maybe after the tenth time Koan refused to discuss it; that nothing had happened. That the days kept coming.

In front of six or seven of us, he just closed his face against it. I knew, then, that the others would start to ask me questions. Goes to show how deep in it we were, that it took all that time.

By then we'd asked him not only as a group but one on one. Queried him about the mountains unshaken, the uncracked sky.

Soon it became their habit to come and find me after they'd been speaking with him, wanting to talk about this 'heated' quality he now had to him, an especial sharpness whenever they asked was there really much harm in *revisiting*, in *reconsidering*. Whenever they asked if things might now go another way.

A way beyond the decisions Koan had made for us. That we had, to be sure, asked him to make for us. But why was he so angry – that's what they wanted to know, why was he so angry?

I didn't point out that he'd always been angry, just that now he showed it more. In his eyes, a raw kind of glimmer. If you looked at him at the right time, you could see it: a hard gleam sweeping.

He never let me forget that I asked him to come here.

Never let me forget my own logic: that it would be better, here.

That we'd have more space. More control. That it would be safer.

That someone like Koan conjured a certain comfort; someone who's well versed and always speaking.

That was what I told him, at least. Truth is I've known there was something prehistoric in me since I was nine and I felt it coming back to me the moment I saw that man on our lawn.

A feeling I was born into and that pre-dated my own human body, that I understood moved of its own accord and would use me as its host for as long as I was living. I realized this when I was nine because that was the year my sister caught a fever and when my father came out of her bedroom I wanted to suck the fingers he'd taken her pulse with.

He came out of the room and though I'd been able to see, from the hall, how he'd stooped over her, seen the tilt of his head as he looked at his watch, I didn't know if he'd pressed on her neck or her wrist to gauge her heart's tempo. I just knew these were the places the heart makes itself known, and that when sickly it fell into a fast, faltering rhythm.

That evening was when it started: when my red was sewn. Not that it had a name. Not that we could see it. But that's what it was, what I felt when my father came out of the room with my sister's pulse still alight on his fingers. Wasn't until years later that it became about the mark a person made – could be sweat or spit or blood. Then that became the real prize: to touch something that had at one time been inside another body.

When I was older I'd go walking in the woods and put my mouth to a tree to catch sap where it was trickling. These two things that looked so different, I knew in my body were one and the same. A man with his lips parted against a tree; a boy in a hallway, wondering at the blood dancing in his sister.

Now that I know how it works there are moments I wonder how it didn't surface before.

Like the night I found the stain on the path only five minutes from the commune, a damp stain that I put my hand to; the shudder when my palm sank into the irony dirt. I knew what it was because I'd been near to a birth before and had seen what happens to a woman's body in the throes, knew that the maternal side of placenta looks like a terrible violence. Knew the mark it could leave behind.

The colour of this smear on the ground: the skin of a bruised, too-ripe plum.

Soft, when I touched it, had made soft, too, the brittle dirt.

Was it one of our women who'd had to hide her stomach and could hide it no longer, who gave birth in the woods hiding from Koan? Or was it some stranger, passing?

Either way, I let myself kneel where a woman's body had been and put my dirtied hand to my face: once more my parents' son.

What eventually did it: one night, after we left, after Beth was born, I tasted Tabatha's milk. She was asleep and I was feeding Beth and after I wiped her mouth clean with my thumb I put it to my own bottom lip. Shudder run through me. Taking inside myself sweet, sweet milk not meant for me. Took a part of Tabatha inside of myself and held it there. Tasted and swallowed her.

Something we still don't know: why it shows up where it does on a given body.

The first time it happened, Tabatha put her hand on my back and said

– I think this is where you've been carrying it. Your fear of what would happen if you gave in. Your fear of your own desires.

What happens when you take off the muzzle?

The moments when I gave in to my dogged perversion and shook with pleasure.

Realized there was nothing to be frightened of, and something else grew in the space the fear left behind.

Koan must truly be sick if all he does is sit in that house. If he knows I've come back and hasn't come out here to gloat, ask me to tell him at length and in detail how we fared better without him – that's not an opportunity the man I know would miss. But then the Koan I lived here with wasn't the Koan I knew from before, so maybe it's not sickness that's changed him. Maybe he's just shed another skin.

Not that he changed all by himself. We all let so much happen. Too much happen. And too often I let Koan have his way.

I did try, before we left.

Told him to imagine what would happen if Eula came back and found out he'd done anything to either of her children.

Even though he thought for sure that Eula was dead, I'm

sure he's been living with the fear since she left; what Eula would say and what Eula would do, if she ever came back.

At the time: thinking it wasn't worth the energy, bringing him to heel. Thinking there were more worthy things to spend our time on.

Tabatha said for that, at least, we should forgive ourselves. Said she still didn't think any of us realized the damage that it did, being told the world you're living in is dying and then living inside the waiting.

The waiting itself a death.

Elena-Vaye told me she once made some red on the woodland floor and that, after, whenever she came close to it, it'd get wet again. Wetter and wetter, she said.

– Like a dog. You know when a dog is happy to see you?

I hadn't believed her, then. But, years later, one morning after Tabatha had fed Beth and her red tears came she used her sleeve to wipe them away, and a week later when she put the shirt back on the cuffs turned wet again.

I should've brought her shirt with me. I'd know by those red cuffs whether or not she was close by.

Whatever they've done to her, I wonder if they went through her things before or after. Wonder how much they know. But their heads are like their stomachs, now. Immune to what's good for them.

And now I'm to do what? Tell them all the things they should know and hope they can hear me? I've been living the truth a long time and there are nights I wake up sick with it. Chest a drum, heart a fist.

I don't know if they can even read, so it might not matter whether or not they found it.

That letter. Ink blooming on Tabatha's thumb.

But if they've seen it, found it, for now at least they won't tell me.

Have to remind myself it's a long, long time they've been living here. That they were *born* here.

I think the coal and its slow burn have set the pace for time passing, and that every year that's passed has counted double. The fumes stopping their bodies from working the way they should.

Now that I'm here, I realize I'd thought they were dead. Makes me think about how desperate we were to leave, all of a sudden. Overnight. Once we knew we were leaving we couldn't believe we'd stayed so long. Didn't matter how we did it, didn't matter what it looked like.

We all accepted it, in different ways, that in leaving them behind we were leaving them to die.

I wonder if they know it themselves, how exactly they've managed to survive.

Anna

The feel of the horse, *at last,* beneath me.
  What a tree knows when it's falling.
  What a she-wolf knows when she's savaging her brood.
  What makes a snake rear back, show you her belly.

Adam

Walking outside and the sun still has a ways to climb. The stones crumble to pebbles, in places. Could the fire be spreading wide enough that we'll someday feel it in the house? Maybe by the time Storm comes, smoke will be drifting out of the unused drain.

It's his legs I see first, the back ones folded – the ankles crossed. Jacob with his stomach falling away from itself. Steam rising and ruby red staining the chalky ground – a red that is blood. It lands with a pang at the back of my throat. I kneel beside him but won't look at his face where I know the eyes are open, large and smooth, the snout flecked with grey, with getting old.

With my hands on the still-hot mound of some plum-coloured organ I feel the woods at my back. The close dark of the trees and the things they hide. What came and hurt him? Some runt a herd left behind that's been wandering around the woods, alone? Or, just as likely, an animal that was simply larger than him, made cruel with being lonesome. Cruel, because he's not been eaten.

He's still all here.

Pleasure-kill.

Thick peaty smell of the fire dampening, making muggy the air, the whole morning sullied with the damp under floorboards, the damp understairs.

The sun shimmers through a sparser patch of cloud and I watch the blood on his coat come alive.

Why kill an old horse?

I stand up and it pains the weak muscles of my knees.

The smell of him coming off my hands. Not just the blood but whatever was in his stomach, the sweet grass he grazed on while he made slow blinks with his heavy eyes.

A noise behind me sets my chest and stomach cramping, but it's Anna standing beside me and I'm crying, for the dead horse and for how empty I feel, how tired. She takes my hand and Jacob's blood is warmed afresh on her palm.

– We'll have to burn him.

A heap of meat this size – if we don't burn him who knows what'll come by.

– We need to take him away from the house.

I open my mouth but there's only the small clicking sound of my throat tightening.

– All right, go inside.

Into the kitchen and closing the door but still I hear him being hacked into smaller pieces that my sister can carry. Smelling the smoke, the meat-tinged smoke from the fire she'll have built a short distance away. When all is quiet I know she's gone to the stream and is rinsing the blood away, has gone into its deep centre and ducked down until the water covers her shoulders. My sister who I lie alongside, my sister with a patch of skin beneath her chin that, no matter the weather, is never dry or chapped, is always smooth. Her cheeks that flame the same colour as her lips when she's been a long time running. When she comes back she's naked aside from the gun. Her hair is wet and pushed back from her face and she carries her dress in her fist, a wet and wrinkled ball. Matthew has come. He looks at each of us, at the mark Jacob made on the ground. Anna won't move her face toward him. To me, she says

– Are you ready?

We kneel down together.

Matthew:

– What happened?

Hot sun rising.

I say

– You know I wouldn't hurt that old horse.

Nothing. She says nothing. And then,

– We are waiting, Storm. Storm, we are waiting.

In my palm: her heartbeat dancing.

Matthew, again,

– What got it? What got the horse?

Again, I say

– Anna, I wouldn't.

A shadow passing over us makes me hopeful: not Storm, but maybe a raincloud – rain, at last, come. But no.

Only another sliver of black smoke, pulsing, eating up more of my vision.

Anna

Poor Jacob. All he did was be a horse.

Koan
Vol. 102
#52

Before Matthew and the others, before the city and after my parents died, my work entailed an awareness of certain practices; what we might call *ritual habits*. I would often travel to certain places to see certain people whose behaviours might be documented, collected, harvested. It wouldn't be right to say that some of them were tedious, but certainly some were more surprising than others.

The *most* surprising was a small community in a notably lush foothill, where they'd developed a technique to train the adolescents for wartime. The technique translated loosely as 'light, swinging', and entailed asking the children to train their eyes on a flame as it was swung in a large circle around the room. Once they were absorbed in tracking the arc of light they became supplicant, dormant, though their bodies carried on moving with great focus and precision.

Since the discovery of the technique, this community had won all its territorial wars. Even in the midst of all that noise, in the throes of violence, their young fighters never felt compelled to flee or even slow their gait.

I went to figure out what was actually happening. What drugs were being slipped to the young men and women, what naturally occurring steroids they were unknowingly imbibing in their tea.

But there was nothing of that kind, and more than twenty years later it still remains remarkable to me that an entire community rotated on an axis so rudimentary.

Six, seven times I watched it performed myself. I watched a woman set a bunch of long, very dry grass ablaze and make quick, crackling circles. She told me, when the rhythm was just right, *Five sweeps is all it takes to put them under.* She wore a coarse, protective glove but from her forearm to her shoulder I could see where the embers had caught her, the skin on that part of her arm like a strangely stippled sleeve.

All those young eyes open; watching the fire swing. Inside each iris: a sliver of flame.

Slowly and with much gestural translation I managed to ask the adolescents if they remembered anything of what came to pass, either in the room with the fire or in the field, and again through fractured clauses the answer came back.

There is a place, at such times, where you can go.

I've been remembering those people, the swinging fire and her pockmarked arm, because I've been trying to think of a way I might do a kindness to the children. How to give them some reprieve from this vicious world we live in. How to soften the edges, quiet the hum. And, if we are to carry on living here for quite some time, how to make them, themselves, a little quieter, a little softer? The *strain* they have caused me; Eula, Matthew. How much more smoothly the years would have run, without their needling.

*

And then, last night, I dreamt a long dream of riding a horse through the nearby hillside. There were countless paths all around us, and all bar the one we trotted down on were poorly kept and overgrown. The horse was wearing blinkers, those thick swathes of leather, and inside the dream I was confused to see them on a horse that wasn't racing.

But when I woke, I knew.

I knew in the way I often do, when I've had time to sleep on a problem.

It was there before me, like a note pinned to the wall.

A tame horse will trot smoothly down any path it's pointed on.

No one thinks the horse has been dealt a cruelty; the unnecessary has simply been curtailed, the excess trimmed from its vision.

And this is all it is: a matter of honing their glances. Of slowly whittling all other paths away – or rather, the suspicion that there are other paths to walk down.

Already I'm sure of it, how quickly it'll bear fruit, because it in fact takes very little for habits to calcify in a human child. Of all the mammals, our infants linger longest in their helplessness. Resolutely suggestible and prone, especially supple and malleable.

Looking at the children here, I find myself thinking more and more of that brief spate of Stone Age hominids with their shocking cranial capacity – their heads that emerged so large and solid from the womb. Superior race, long extinct. Their spines were not so rubbery as ours, their instincts more assured. It's estimated they would have been walking within a few months, had they survived, if they had not – on account of their size – been born to mothers unable to swaddle, nurse and coo. Evolution's wheels are sometimes determined to turn slow and so we've not seen any amendments, since – the species, it seems, is incapable of producing a robust child that doesn't decimate its mother's pelvic floor. Or, incapable of producing a female that can withstand such a birth.

As such; we've been left with our fragile, precious heads – the membrane and bone that take such time to suture, and a pocket of flesh you could rupture with a pinprick. Tamper with the head and you see a whole person undone.

That pocket of flesh is what I keep my eye on, when the boy is singing.

Under his hair; a sea urchin, shivering.

He comes to see me almost every day while his mother and sister are sleeping. If someone were to ask him what we do in the house, these days, he'd report quite simply that I've taught him a song, and every day I ask him to sing it.

What he wouldn't say is that I ask him to sing it with his eyes closed and to sing very quickly, at the beginning, and then to gradually slow. He wouldn't say that while he's singing I light a lantern that's hung from the ceiling and set it spinning so that its beam circles the room.

Once he's eased into his wakeful sleeping I start giving him tasks to do.

Simple, simple tasks.

Fill and empty your cup, Adam.

And, while he's warmed and calm,

Redness is the scourge of Storm.

You must scorch your own heart, pluck out your own tongue, if that's where you feel a red thought coming.

Very, very simple. Things that are straightforward, self-evident, with the ring of something you already know.

The longer we wait for Storm, the sweeter Her arrival.

And then later I set down a candle and he passes his finger through the flame. If, in his sleep-state, he either fumbles or declines there's a small, quick punishment. The barest hint of violence, just enough to prickle the senses. The smell of hair singeing, for instance, is hugely effective. It takes no time at all to cut a snippet of his hair and burn it, keeping the chemical smell right up close to his face. And then, with his nostrils flaring, I'll tell him, again,

> *Carmine, ruby, garnet, puce – when you see it you start running.*
> *Salt your hands and wash out your eyes when you see the red man coming.*

Today, when he left, I heard him singing his way back to the cottages.

> *I saw a red bird and it had a red beak and its babies were all far flung,*
> *I saw a red cat and all its red kittens had been left out in the sun.*

It takes so, so little, to do a kindness. To soften terrors and suffuse a child's wakeful moments with calm.

Matthew

What Eula and I had in common. We could each see in the other something people should steer clear of. Some of the things that woman told me: shocking just for being said out loud. The things she could admit to herself without flinching. One day, out of nowhere,

– I shouldn't be a mother.

I told her lots of women feel that way until it's happening, or until the children are grown, but she was adamant. Said she'd been told she couldn't have children when she was young. Said she wanted them, badly, for years, but came around to it eventually and started living her life in a very particular way. And of course, soon as she realized she was having them the world was ending. Huffing out her nose when she said it, which was, mostly, her way of laughing.

Then she asked me if I could remember Adam crying all the time, when he was born, and when I said no more than a normal baby she said no, I had to remember that it was all the time, said

– I left him in the woods. So help me I took him into the woods and laid him down and then I went and stood with my back to him, maybe thirty feet away, and I waited for him to die. It had been cruel to begin with, bringing them into the world. Seemed crying was his way of telling me he didn't want to be here.

178

Her chest marked with a fresh scratch where a branch had swung back at her.

– What happened?

– Well, the crying stopped. So I was certain, then. That he'd died.

Massaging her knees and thighs. Rubbing some tincture into them. Forbidden dash of vanity, tending to the skin of her legs, keeping them soft.

– I turned around and there was a deer, standing over him, and she was licking him. That's what had stopped him crying.

She stopped talking then but I knew what she was thinking.

A comfort that small, that unspectacular. But still; a comfort she couldn't provide.

And then taking a handful of ash and rubbing her feet with it, toughening her soles. Looking at me with those quick, icy eyes that have landed in her daughter. No way to know with either of them if they're telling the truth. All you ever see of them is what they want you, at that particular moment, to be seeing.

I told her I wasn't the sort of person who should be most things, certainly not a parent, and she'd said

– But you've got a handle on it. You know when to keep away.

From people, she meant. People who I was likely to gulp down without realizing.

A rare burst of kindness in a woman so hard. Though I don't know if she'd have said it had she known, someday, it'd be me coming back here. To find her children.

*

179

Took Eula no time at all to find us. Not so surprising, really, that we'd all been living close all that time.

She'd thought, of course, her children were with us. When she realized she made Tabatha say it, over and over,

Your children, your children . . .

But of course, they're not children. Just more young people who'll never be properly grown. And it's too late, now – they're callused to nourishment. Even if they some- how had a proper meal I don't think their stomachs could stand it.

Would be enough to break anyone, was what Tabatha kept saying, *it'd be enough to break anyone, hearing it all at once.*

And she's right.

But seeing them here now, seeing how they've been living – I'm not sure how much else there is to break, if there's any point doing this dance with them.

I know the jellyfish are a good sign, a solid sign, and if it had come five years ago – three years even – we might have still had the energy – to make sense of it, to be surprised. But it seems crueller somehow, to tell them. It'll be a whole 'nother world that we're asking them to live in.

Though it puts a fear in me, just imagining saying the words to her: *Eula, your children are broken.*

Anna knows more than she's letting on but she's still fixed on Storm. That part hasn't gone away.

But she's preoccupied with other things. The *work* she does, pretending that boy is sane.

Swallowed it like a glass of milk, him getting up in the night to gut that horse. I found the blade where he tossed it, a blade I've seen him use to skin the rabbits. He cried and he cried, and she put her hand to the back of his head.

Wouldn't look at me, just kept her hand there, cupped his skull until the sun was fit to burn her. I told her I wouldn't go until I could see she'd gone to bed and how she looked at me, then. Though I've said it before and only half meant it, the way she turned to me: Eula. Without baring her teeth, letting me know it'd cost her nothing at all to bite me. *She* has all of Eula's force and at least a little of her easy cruelty, and *he* caught all her madness.

Or maybe he caught only a trace of it, and it's been this time with Koan that saw it turn solid inside him. Those hours he spent alone with him – the damage I can only guess at atop the damage I know for certain.

If Eula had been here, this morning. If she'd seen it herself.

Him covered in the blood of that wretched animal. Her stroking the back of his head, like it was any other morning.

Koan
Vol. 150
#94

Things have started to wear on Matthew.

He comes to see me often, when he knows I'm otherwise occupied and wants to discuss what could have happened – see if we might, together, account for the delay. I'm not sure when he lost it: the ability to hide his agitation. All I can tell him is what I myself do, which is take comfort in the fact that none of this was ever *predictable*. That it'll take the time it takes. That there's no point in wearing himself out with fretting.

– Wasn't the whole point of coming here – of you wanting to come here – wasn't it to wait it out in a dignified way?

– We were meant to be here six months, maybe eight.

At first, it was once a year that he would come to me and do this: sit with his head in his hands, kneading at the flesh around his eyes. Now a month doesn't go by without him coming here and asking the same questions over and over. All our old training, all our old knowledge lifted off his tongue. He sounds like any other man, now. Weak as any other man.

– What does that mean, Matthew? 'Meant to be'? When was the last time a phrase like that proved useful to you?

But he couldn't be distracted. An extra heat in him, today. Extra dose of fever.

– Something has happened, since. Something must have happened.

– Plenty is happening all the time.

– There's no way we could have been so far off.

– You're right. Of course you're right. There's no possibility we got it wrong, so all that's happening is that it's taking longer.

– But *this* much longer, Koan—

– Yes. This much longer.

– I want to go and see what's happened.

I couldn't help but wonder if he was dreaming up a reason to leave. If he's simply tired of being accountable to all these other people.

– Just wait a little longer. Do this one thing for me, and wait a little longer.

– Not just me you need to ask. Eula and the others, they're jittery.

He was sitting by now, his back rounded against the wall.

– They're jittery and I can't blame them.

– Sounds like Eula is fashioning a mutiny.

– I know you don't like Eula but you can't deny – she's strong.

– Your point?

– People like that. Like being near a person stronger than them, saves them making their own choices.

His palms covering the whole of his face, his fingers an electric white where they slipped into his hair.

– I'm ready for it, Koan.

The things we all went through, to get here. Not just to this place, but to a state resembling calm. A near-constant quiet: no sudden screams, no jolts of realization like a rush of cold water. Everyone going about the day and the night, and all the while simply *accepting*. People like Matthew, I think, accepted it faster. People who were born into the world in a particular way, when they heard it was ending – I think they felt a release. I think they felt *About time*.

From behind his hands:

– Hell. Gotten to the stage I want it.

And I told him what I know, though it's difficult to pinpoint the exact moment it became true.

– We all want it. We're all ready.

Adam

Today 'round noon I went there, to his old home, and stood close to the last full wall, thinking that I'd hear him move or that he'd appear in the doorway and ask if he can come to our cottage and be properly inside. But nothing.

There's a thin tree growing there but it's not enough to give him any kind of shelter. If I mention it to Anna I know she'll just say *Night-timer.* Meaning *Of course he can tolerate a little discomfort, a little cold.*

Dusk comes and he's there right away, so we know he's been waiting. The pot on the fire is where I left it, bubbling. He starts talking at Anna. She cuts him off, says

– Going to see Koan?

– Yes, but I want to talk with you first.

– We can talk after.

– Anna.

Anna's hard breath. Matthew's mouth fighting to keep its stillness.

The old pot between us carries on gleaming.

Its buffered, bulbous body. Strange flickering moment feeling sick over all the things I ever thought to eat. It can't be true that they don't carry on living, at least a little, inside us. The rabbits and their noses, twitching.

Now the pot is gleaming so bright I don't know how

they don't shield their eyes from it. A little child-moon landed between us with a mind to scorch our vision.

I want to say out loud what she means: *Storm is coming and that is our world entire.*

Instead, all I say:

– Look.

Silver planet rising.

The three of us kneel down to make devotion. Tonight I'm in the middle, so Matthew's and Anna's hands are interlaced across my neck and though I can't tell whose fingers are whose I can tell without looking that Matthew keeps quiet while showing Storm his crown.

I wake up early because I'm thirsty. I can see right away, coming outside, that there hasn't been rain. Some of the soil so dry it's taken on a tint of copper.

Downstairs, Matthew is already there scratching at his shoulders and I think of his tender skin, too porous – the pores flaming.

There's a lack of sleep showing in the clay colour to his mouth and the grey smudge to his eyes that sits so thick on his skin I wonder if he's daubed them with ashes. Old, private ritual night-timers sometimes carried out at dusk around the fire.

His shirt almost crackles as he pulls it around him, the heavy salt dried tough in the fibre.

Dried out by the fire he sits near to, but never beside.

– You want another shirt, Matthew? Something softer?

I look at his hands, at the skin that coats the knuckles – flaking.

– Koan used to say he could tell when the women were

close to birth. Said they'd make a pile of anything even slightly soft.

I don't say anything, use a spoon to take some stray innards out of the still-cooking broth. Flick them on the ground.

– For *nesting*, he said. Because they knew they'd need soft things for nesting. He said women turned just a little bit animal, before. Deep down in their mammal core, was what he said, deep down in their animal history, they knew what they'd soon be needing. He said they didn't even notice they were doing it. After he told me I saw it, too – things that didn't even belong to them they'd take. A shirt you'd been taking good care of, a not-too-old sheet off a line.

He'd be speaking this way even if he was sitting here alone. Still, I say

– All those births and no children.

His face; the twitch across his mouth, his eyes. Something in his body paining him.

– People tried to avoid it happening. Some of the children, if they'd twinned, would have been the same age as you – were inside of their mothers before any of us knew . . . but. Well. It happens. It happened here what, four, five times? By the end whoever was having the baby didn't want Koan to know . . . it got complicated.

First spark on the horizon, bright shimmer catching in my good eye.

Matthew is leaning forward. His weight making tilt the seat.

– I'm not sure that I can make it clear to you. What it was like. That happening over and over.

The sun'll sit high, today. I can feel it already: the earth warming.

– If we'd known that—

But Anna comes out of the cottage and he stops talking. She moves straight for the stones and we follow her, our knees lined up on the ground.

– Come, Storm, and make us whole. Make us whole, Storm, come.

Matthew

When Beth came out of Tabatha: roseate palms, one iris swollen and puce. We put her in the bed between us and, from time to time, I would put my mouth on the soft dent of her scalp and say what we had said to one another before she was born.

– You have been a risk worth taking.

But there was no risk. Only a small human who was somehow the exact weight and shape of my own heart. All of a sudden I had a heart, again. Four chambers full of blood and breath and they were moving.

That night, with the afterbirth on the path – I heard a woman singing.

It was low and it was throaty and though it was tender it made me feel afraid and though it made me feel afraid I followed the sound of it.

I probably thought what I was about to see would make me feel better; what could be sinister about a woman singing?

Funny how some lessons take years – decades – to learn.

Not far into the woods, a place where the trees were leafless and the brush had started to thin.

Sitting with her back to me, the curve of it. The V of

her open knees. In front of her, her ankles would be crossed, their outer bones wedged into the dirt.

She turned her face to one side, and though she couldn't see me she knew – knew us all by scent.

– Do you know this song, Matthew?

– What's happened?

– Only the usual, only the inevitable.

I took another step – stopped myself. My eyes suddenly tired with the things they'd seen and that I wished I could lift out of them.

She turned away from me again. Spoke straight ahead.

– It seemed the least I could do, to sing to it.

– I'm sorry, I—

– Don't be sorry. I simply could not let it happen.

– What do you mean?

– I mean I closed my eyes and thought of a wall of red bricks falling down. For hours that was all I let myself think of, and then I felt things start to move.

– Jesus Christ, Eula—

– There's all sorts of ways to be a mother.

She couldn't have been far along. I'd noticed nothing, there'd been no sign.

– Was there a father?

Which made her laugh: loud and unafraid in the dark. I thought *I could live my whole life and never meet another person with so little fear in her.*

– There was a man in the right place at the right time.

Someone in our group, someone passing on the road?

– Although probably to him it didn't feel that way.

It's not something I could picture: being caught in the snare of Eula's desire. *Desire* was probably the wrong word

190

for it. Probably it would go by another name, if a man did it to a woman.

– And you're not worried?

That, after this thing that had happened – this strange, sad thing – her red would come.

– I only did what I knew to be right and what my body told me to do.

Those parts where the rest of us are permeable, where we would fall to the ground if punctured – here Eula was made of stone that would never shatter. I could see it: her pelvis, her ribcage. All of it swept with concrete and marble.

– Leave us be now, Matthew.

Walking away I heard it start behind me again, the singing. A tune I didn't, in fact, know. Not that this was in itself unusual, my childhood having mostly been void of song. The lack of music and play – these things that I'd thought, in simpler times, made my childhood a cruel one.

The top of her spine rising out of her neck was still seared on my vision, when Tabatha told me there was another baby inside Eula. That was what I saw: Eula's neck bent as she sang into her lap, to the morsel of muscle she'd willed out of herself.

All sorts of ways to be a mother.

That crescent of flesh was partly why I said, right away,

– Yes, whatever happens we cannot stay. Yes, we will go.

I'll know more when I go see Koan.

Koan, who's apparently been sick since we left. Maybe sick since I last went to see him, and we both said and did things we'd like to undo.

191

When I think of the hot anger he put in me with just a few deft phrases.

When I think of the feel of him, his hair and his skin.

There are things I'm not proud of but couldn't have helped and things I might've prevented if I'd worked a little harder.

I'm not sure which kind it was, the last time I saw Koan.

I shouldn't be here, alone with them. I shouldn't be alone with anyone who isn't Tabatha.

When my father came out of my sister's room he touched my shoulder. I was young enough that he could take the entire shoulder in one hand and he grasped me in that thoughtless, familiar way a father sometimes will with his children. When he did it I felt my sister's pulse land there; just for a moment it fluttered inside me. Later, whenever I felt my thoughts getting too much for me Tabatha would knead that part of my body, work into it with her elbow and fist.

– All it is, she'd say, is a sore tired muscle.

She thought too highly of me, and no one thought highly enough of her.

That's the thing I should have told her.

That's the exact thing I should have said.

But turns out I can't go to Koan tonight.

I've lost track of the days; I feel it coming.

That time again.

part iii

Shedding Velvet

Think of it: a roaring that goes on and on. A wave that is an open mouth, that is never silent.

Think of the rush of the foam, the sound of the foam.

Think of a wave that is rising like a voice is rising.

Think of a wave that can do what a voice can do: call out, scream, shout.

Adam

Dusk is coming on and I go looking for Matthew. All his talk of newborns, something left in the hollow of my ear; prickling.

There's mist this evening and it settles silver and thick around the cottages, each of them worn down to a little ruin. The walls pared back to roughshod peaks and the windows jagged and wide. With the roofs fallen in, when it rains you can hear the droplets sliding down their inside walls and pattering on their inside tables, and when the sun shines on to them the light is made fall in hard, overlapping lines. Sometimes during the too-long days that come with summer I'll come and lie down here, where the moss has made a blanket of the floor, pretend I'm waiting on the others to get back from the stream – everyone coated with a mineral scent. But it isn't summer, it's only spring, and so the mist is a cold one and leaves a breath of moisture on my shins.

I see him just as his old ruined home comes into view.

He's crouching in such a way that his gut must be cramping.

Only, as well as crouching, his shoulders are churning and he's rolling his neck side to side, his face pointing now up, now down. Bouncing on his ankles, breathing loud.

He's sick, very sick. What could he have eaten? He's eaten nothing that we didn't eat. Mother used to tell us to be mindful of swallowing the tiny wriggling creatures that live in the stream but has he even been near the water since he got here?

And where'd he get that old red shirt?

Why's he taking it off like that, trying to shrug it off his back?

But no piece of cloth would make that stale, papery sound.

Long and shapeless, folding into itself and tearing when it touches the ground.

That's what's making the sound, that crackling.

Red.

Red.

Red this whole time.

And now, in the cool of the evening, when he must be feeling some relief, he's sloughing off his red skin that leaves behind a back that is too unmarked, the same colour all over. Not the skin of a man his age. Not the shoulders of a person who lived part of their life in the sun. Even Anna's skin is a little mottled where clear, a little pockmarked where smooth.

When he turns to look at me I expect his whole face will be copper and twisted but it's still his face, his mouth ringed with the same stubbled groove. I mean to run but my calves only jolt inside their skin.

He stands up and turns toward me so I can't quite see it but I know it's there, behind him.

Puce shroud.

Carmine veil.

Ruby cloak.

– I haven't known how to tell you.

It's the first time I've seen his shoulders without his shirt. How did we miss it? That this part of his body was never nude.

– It doesn't mean what we thought it did.

Showing me his sex, his mouth. Hiding his shoulders, which are too smooth. Unbroken water.

– Do you hear what I'm saying?

Red seeds make red roots of a red tree you'll soon be climbing.

My throat closing, stomach rising.

The red man means to lie down beside you.

His eyes jump and I know that he's seen Anna and that she'll have raised her gun.

The red man wants to live under your skin, taste with your tongue, see with your eyes.

– There was a lot we got wrong.

I feel the heat of my sister beside me, come to look at Matthew turned to poison before us.

– Think of it like a rash, or a mix of a rash and a scar.

His throat as broad and thick as the most muscled part of my arm.

– There's a letter. When Tabatha came, she had a letter.

I look at Anna but she's still gazing her slow gaze at Matthew, who must know, though he's talking, though he's thinking hard, what's only a few moments away from happening.

The red man is slippery with crude desires.

– The way you were brought up, it's not your fault.

Steadying himself, still trying.

– Way we left you. We're to blame.

Red wind, red rain, red hurricane.

199

Anna says

– Do you want to kneel or do you want to turn around?

Now his face is buckling.

My tongue is a slug, fat and slow, and I'll be sick if I have to look at him and his snakeskin a moment longer. The coarse hair of his sex, the tough skin of his chest and the smooth of his back; all of him, gleaming, because on top of the mist a light rain has started.

Now, at last, we've rain.

– You're still only children, in a lot of ways. You know that, don't you?

Anna raises the gun on to her shoulder.

He takes a half-step toward us. I know he means to say *Please. Don't.*

But all he says is

– No.

She shoots him and it makes the usual sound. Because he's a tall man, when he hits the ground the soil rises up quite a ways. I can see the soil, but not him. He's hidden by the cottage's worn-down wall. Anna walks past me, over toward it, stays still a few moments. I hear a choking sound, which I know will stop eventually. Anna moves inside the cottage to peer at the pile of skin.

– What to do with this?

Though we already know.

Burn it.

And put it in a hole in the ground, if it resists flame.

Think now: is such a wave something you would ever feel compelled to step inside? And why not? Can you put words to it? To the terror of being inside a wave that is always, always rising?

Anna

I told Adam how painful it would be but he'd gone up into his head. Gone behind his sick eye.

I pulled my brother into the understairs room and scoured him, made him cry. Made him gag after wadding little crystals down the sides of his gums. Dabbing it along his lashes, taking extra time with his bad eye. Not long until there were welts forming, raised blotches and streaking lines.

On and on I kept rubbing.

Never before have we been so close to one of them – so close and for so long and he touched the both of us. His hand on me. And Adam saying something about Matthew's mouth, Matthew's tongue.

When it was my turn Adam could hardly move for how sore he was. He looked like something had stopped halfway through eating him alive. I showed him my bent back and said *Hard as you can, Adam*. Told him *Harder, harder* and I knew he was going hard enough only when my own eyes were watering and my mouth tasted like iron. I did my own chest and legs, daubed my face up so tight the salt in my mouth mixed with salt coming down the back of my nose. Crusted mask I had to peer through.

Any time I felt myself wavering I thought of that hand on me and that sweep of skin he was shedding.

The veil, which I burned myself.

No need for Adam to see it shrivelling.

Who knows, as it is, what this'll spark in him, what he'll do. But at least I know he won't ask any of the questions a healthy, wakeful person would be asking. Won't be asking

How didn't we know?

What letter?

But, all the same.

The pleasure it gave me.

To shoot him.

Hear his tall body hit the ground.

Koan
Vol. 150
#95

I couldn't get back to work, after Matthew left. He leaves the shape of himself behind him so that, sitting at my desk to write, I still felt cornered by his long torso, his big shoulders. And so I gave in, went walking. Took my favourite path by the farrow room which leads to a track where no one goes. Looking at the plants, the red-veined sorrel whose whole leaf and stem are now, also, crimson, the buckwheat which used to flower white, the dandelion no longer yellow.

And then: I came upon a wounded crow. Snagged in the carmine lavender with one wing folded beneath her. Such hysterical sounds she made, when I lifted her. The way the botched limb shuddered in its joint when she tried to summon it into flight.

I held her and I thought of Eula with her hip for ever grating in the joint. I thought of Eula, who never lets me come close to her, never acknowledges when she needs assistance or aid. I thought of Eula running into the woods and Matthew speaking into his palms, saying her name.

One thing that confused me, when we first arrived: all the little cages.

So many of the cottages had them, and always in a different room. I didn't dwell on it because, at that time, a community of pet birds seemed a very paltry strangeness. But when I realized I didn't know how I'd missed it: parakeets.

Birds kept close because of the fumes they unwittingly measure.

And then it had seemed a shame to me, so many cages empty – it dampened my humour whenever I remembered they were there. Some metal, some wooden. Their small doors open, the hooks they hung from squeaking.

The strength of her jolting inside my hands when she saw the cage, as though she knew what it meant. I thought *Even a wild bird knows a cage when she sees one*. I thought I'd be driven demented by the sound of her trying to fight her way out from inside it. I thought she'd break the other wing and wondered if it would sit at the same awkward angle.

But already, after a week, she's grown used to her life there, the floor of her suspended home matted with her feathers and her droppings. I let her out and again and again with her crooked-healing wing she flies into the corner, for some reason thinking that's the way out – that part of the room where the ceiling meets the wall. She's made the paint there grey and sooty but I don't mind. For hours at a time, she'll brutalize herself against the beams and the rafters. And then she'll collapse, exhausted. Either I lift her or she returns herself to the cage.

I've come to see it as an omen for a good day, the times she goes back, unassisted.

The bad wing seems to make her fly in uneven circles; she'd never survive, back outside.

She'd die instantly and she knows it.

She hates for me to see her eat the seeds I bring her, but

I hear her. I hear her beak against the floor of the cage as soon as I leave the room. She's starving – she doesn't want me to see it but I know it; she's starving all the time.

Today the boy came to see me.

I said

– How's your sister? How's your mother?

And he said they were doing just fine, that his mother had tracked a deer and they were going to eat it.

– Well, she'll have to share with everyone.

And he nodded, said he knew.

– Even your mother has to follow the rules.

To which he said nothing, just sat down and looked at some old instruments I'd left out on the table. A syringe, a scalpel. I saw his eyes linger over my journal, my handwriting which reads to him as impenetrable code.

He went under especially easy, today, and I thought *Why not take him to see my crow? Let him watch her butchered flight?* I let him sing for another ten minutes, just to be certain, and then I lifted him by the arms and nudged him by the shoulders – he moved for me so easily, compliant and docile as water.

I stood him right at the cage, and then I opened it, let the bird panic her way around the room. He didn't stir an inch, just stood there, and it struck me it must be accumulative, this treatment. That he grows more receptive each time. But then I realized he wasn't watching her, so I took his face in my hands and tilted it; told him to count the wingbeats inside her flapping. Told him that was all he had to do. Count the wingbeats as they hit the wall.

Large, black bird with her feather dust falling.

This usually pliable boy resisting me.

He didn't want to look and I kept on holding his face, told him that Storm was inside those beating wings – their numeration and their broken sound, inside of it was Storm, Storm was the very movement of her wings.

I said

– Count them, Adam, count them.

And he did. Inside my hands I felt it, his jaw moving as he clucked the numbers on his tongue.

Afterwards, inside his eye: barely, just barely – a black droplet spreading.

Trace of disobedience. The black drop marking the moment he'd looked away.

When I watched him walk back to the cottages, from behind I could see his elbow jutting out; rubbing, rubbing, rubbing.

Adam

Red Matthew.
    A red man came.

I dream of Anna in the woods – my sister with her strong heart thumping.

She's wading out from the shoreline and there are fleshy creatures strewn about her thin ankles and her callused heels. She kneels down into the water and a mark winds up her arm and over her shoulders. Deft copper twist no wider than twine darting up her scalp, past the rim of her hairline, dark encrusted ruby-mauve and inside of her dress, here and there she is wettening, toughening, rocking to and fro in a way I've never seen before, her hips felled again and again into circles, a broken rhythm only her pale, night-time body knows.

And all the while, that red line – bright and deep: spreading.

Somehow; another dawn. Anna says
    – There it is.
    Meaning the sun.
    We watch the sky turn orange, turn red.
    – Come, Storm, and consume us. Consume us, Storm, come.

Back at the fire and dusting off her knees.

– Adam, stop it.

– What?

– That song.

Sometimes I think she's hearing it inside her head. It follows the both of us; childhood tune.

I saw red mice and they had red tails so I stomped them one
by one,
I saw a red spider and it spun a red web so I squished it with
my thumb.

A high wind passing.

Looking out from the bedroom window and over woodland, down to the sea. Wherever there are flowers they are being made to move by this fast, dry wind.

From the sound of the waves I know they're rolling high and wide. Were we to walk to the shore, we'd be bathed in their spray.

I don't mean to cry. May as well try not to shiver in the wind. Anna comes and puts her arms around me. A warm smell comes from between her flesh and dress and shawl, heady stench that running makes. The day is coming on and she can't stay awake, but she lets me follow her upstairs and lie in bed beside her.

– Just for a little while.

Under the blankets she's sleeping, kicking at the sheets.

Her hair sticking to her face where it is especially damp, warm.

Salt-sore. Every step stinging.

Shape of her feet, their soles are lined with hatching

scars. A pair of eels living in the cold dark at the bottom of a lake. But her neck – her neck is one long, clean feather.

Only time she closes her eyes, to sleep. Not to sing or swallow. Only to sleep.

But even in her sleep she's watching.

It's not dreams that tug her eyes to and fro, but the pattern some distant creature makes in flight.

My face near hers, tasting her sleep-breath. I take hold of her wrist and clench my thighs in time to the jolt in her veins.

Hard hot swell.

The dark to my left side is pulsing, current caught in a rockpool.

Her hand over my face, slow and soft, her fingers troubling the passage of air and so it stays fluttering in my nose and mouth, not letting it come in or out. I think of Matthew: smooth back, red veil. Not long until my chest is hurting, the little bit of breath remaining countless nicks from deft little blades.

My throat roaring like I've been down in the surf, gulping.

Closer and closer, 'til it's all I can feel, that liquid rush, that pulling.

As always when she sleeps her sleep seems to pool out beneath her and to give off, in the curtained light, a sparkling gossamer sheen.

With my head on her stomach I can hear the rabbit and broth rocking inside her. What does that rabbit know about her that I don't? The passage of her throat, her moist, inside-heat. Each part of her a chamber I'd lie down inside, her belly a soft field where I'd sleep long and deep, her collar two sides of a halving moon that'd colour me silver as I lay dreaming.

I tread the crackling hair of her sex and the moisture there sets my bitten fingers stinging. I cover it with the whole of my hand and think of those animals that, sensing danger, believe themselves hidden if they cover their own eyes. I keep my hand there and feel more heat rising, rising, and from some deep, divoted memory a voice saying *Less to fathom, more to hide.* But who would have said such a thing?

Anna comes awake just enough to hold my hand, to still it.

My pulse rising to match hers.

All the blood between us, quickening.

The sheets are twisted tight. Sweet sore warmth that feels like it's dripping from my belly. Her undone braid resting to one side.

– Anna?

A long breath, in and out.

– Yes, Adam?

– Don't you like it?

– Like what?

– Being my sister.

Sigh-sound.

Not breath, this time.

Just the eaves as the sun's early warmth sets them stirring.

Daytime, come again.

I say

– We're like the sun and the moon, passing one another in the sky.

A little more quiet.

I go to the window, look out to the sea.

Her voice, behind me,

– Let's go see Koan.

What is the logic of such a wave? That it can move only up, that it's bound to this ever-upward motion? That it is locked in ascension and can never stop, no matter how hard it might wish to break, no matter how rich with ache the salty water, no matter how appetizing the shore – what is the purpose of such a wave, that knows only how to rise?

Koan
Vol. 193
#9

Matthew walked right in today. No knock and no fore-
warning, so I suppose he's been suspecting something.
Watchful Matthew. Shadowy. Wide-eyed. He does himself
damage by getting up like this in the middle of the day.

Even if he hadn't known before today, when he walked
in the boy was sleeping and so he didn't look around, he
kept entirely still. He said something when he first came in
but I couldn't hear it over the singing. Not that I needed to.

Matthew; no matter what comes to pass he stays angry.
He's always thought his outrage makes him strong. One of
the ways in which he lacks vision, and that lack showed
through today when all he could see was a dazed, chanting
child.

I told him to think of the terror we once felt, that we
had to learn to digest and master, asked what he thought
that would do to a child's body – not only the fear but the
strain of containing it. Growing up under the reign of such
terror. Told him to remember the long nights before we
came here, before we'd come to appreciate the depth and
the majesty of Storm. The children could be spared all of it
with so little effort, hardly any fuss at all. All it is – a matter of letting one light rather than another shine brighter.

Asked him if it wasn't something he'd choose for himself, putting aside for good the things he wished he never knew.

– You're hurting him, was all he said.

And I laughed at his shock over the little patches of altered skin, that he should be so disturbed by these whispers of hurt – tiny oval wounds on his fingers.

– You think a little burn now is worse than what'll happen later, if he's not careful? Better a small scorch he won't even remember.

– Not what I meant.

Looking down, at the top of his head,

– Can't you get him to stop?

The singing, he meant.

I knew what he'd be thinking, by now, and I was ready to hear it, but he only said

– You're too deep in it. You've gone too deep.

– Without us they'd have been birthed like feral kittens on the side of the road.

– Not just this, Koan, all of it. You're too deep in all of it.

And then he left, telling me he wouldn't say anything to anyone so long as today was the last day. Said 'the absolute last', and that he wouldn't tolerate it, not even one more time. I laughed again, that he thinks me moved by what he can and can't endure. And Adam, all the while, despite this tall man towering and his voice rising – he slept right on through.

Anna

But how did we not know?

A shirt all he needed to keep it hidden.

Either Koan left something out or red is changing, has grown, because no matter where his red was showing we should have known by his voice, his eyes – our own bodies should have told us.

And now Adam distracting himself by eating me with his eyes. Something slipped inside, tripping up on itself. An important, meaty part.

This morning when I sat down at the fire there was a black mark near my knee and I thought it was his eyes on me – that it had happened at last, I'd started to wear the toll of him always, always looking.

It was only wet soot from last night's fire but I held my breath 'til it was rubbed away clean.

Coming too close to me.

Too close and too close and closer again.

I knew when I said it, this time, that he would come to see Koan. What happened with Matthew jolted something loose – put a fear in him that he knows, somewhere deep, will only be countered by Koan reciting his old lessons. All the lines and phrases Adam swallowed whole like he was being fed something sweet.

Mother used to say there's a limit to how much you can give a person. Told me

– There's being a good sister and then there's letting someone else live up there on your shoulders.

But I can do this for him; keep him safe until Storm is come. He just needs to stay whole a little longer, and then the ways he's hurt won't matter. He'd do it for me, if I'd been born the sick one.

And while Koan talks at Adam I can look at his journals.

Look properly. Skip ahead.

Bottom-right-corner shelf.

Something in there about red he doesn't want us to know, something he never told us.

Adam

Not since the others left have we walked here together with Anna's wrist looped around mine.

The strong-smelling smoke is dusky blue where it comes out of the hot road. We can see it behind the house, through the trees; puffs of smoke and sickly steam. Every few moments a dash of orange or red which is the fire eating its way up a little further, weakening the ground.

– Remember now, he's frailer than when you last saw him.

– I understand.

– Frailer, stranger.

– I know.

She lets go of my hand because she's too warm and I myself feel queasy, walking here. Probably it's the rain and all the pent-up scent it's releasing. Rich kelp stink from where it's been stewing on the shore.

The house is much as I remember it only darker, and Koan is much as I remember him – only smaller. At first I think he's a pile of laundry been left to dry by the weak fire. It's the fire Anna moves toward, stoking it and brightening the room.

– Look who's come to see you, Koan.

The man inside the clothes turns to me – his face, his chest and shoulders.

– It's Adam, come to say hello.

Her body doesn't look right beside him. If nothing else it seems like she might burn him, just by standing there. Standing next to his old grey flesh makes her seem hotter than the fire. He opens his mouth, and though it can't be so I hear a crisp, tearing sound.

I have my hands on the back of another chair and I grip it, now; my bad eye panging.

– Motherhood didn't suit her. I wondered if you'd come out of her at all.

Anna lets out a long breath, looks at me, says

– That's enough about Mother, Koan.

And now she moves behind him, over to the shelves lined with his journals.

– Have you been devoting yourselves?

She says

– We have.

Turning his face quickly, side to side, as though following a rodent around the room. My dark eye pulses and I sit down in the chair whose back I've been holding. Anna reaches down, pulls out a journal and opens it, begins to turn the pages. If it needed proving he's sick this would be the thing to do it, that she doesn't need to keep the reading hidden.

– Tell him about Matthew, Adam.

Koan looks at me, his eyes too widely open, says

– Matthew . . . Matthew . . . is not a good person.

I wait for Anna to say something else. She can't mean it, that I should tell this sick man what has happened. She looks up from the pages, from Koan's neat hand, and closes the journal – reaches down again, puts it back on the shelf, takes out another. Though the walls of my throat are stinging, I say it:

– Matthew was red.

Koan's lips come together, back apart.

– Red?

With my good eye adjusting to the light I can see that while his skin has lost its colour his hair is still a rich dark brown.

– Yes, I say, Anna shot him.

And he nods to himself, his eyes shining.

– Matthew was a very angry man.

One pale hand comes over the other in his lap. In the bad light they look like spilled milk. Anna puts back the second journal and now she takes out a third. I can't make out her face but know her reading habits: chewing on the side of her mouth, her head nodding to one side.

For the first time since seeing his broad back, since seeing him roll his shoulders, I can take a breath without my chest working to push it away.

Angry Matthew, moving redly through the world.

– I thought she must be eating you.

Koan is looking at me, and I know this is the first time he's really seen me since I came inside.

– I was sure she'd found a way to shave off your limbs as they were growing. Found a way to get strong on your flesh, keep you small.

He's speaking low. Nothing like his old voice that our days were once shaped by. I want to cover my eye, to soothe my sight which is pounding, pounding.

Just barely, I manage to say

– Anna.

– I thought you were dead when you came out. Your

sister was silent but she was looking around. Your face was all shut up, and you wouldn't cry.

Sound of Anna turning a page inside this journal, this last one at which she's been staring.

Slight motion, left to right, as she reads – her face following the tug of her eyes.

– She didn't want me in the room with her, you know. And she wouldn't wear the veil. Told me she'd wrap it 'round my throat. Up until the very last moment she kept her legs closed even though her whole body must have been telling her otherwise.

The sound of wings beating, beating.

– Can you imagine the will of such a woman?

Trapped bird.

Erratic bird.

Blooded droplets strewn behind it, marking the arc of its flight.

– To override with the muscles of her legs every chemical, hormonal instruction? Her shut thighs a wall of stone.

I can feel the stirred air at my ear.

– She told me to stand at her shoulder. Even then, at such a time, she didn't want anyone near that part of her body. I thought having you might soften her. I thought she'd stay still, from time to time. But she carried you both like you were nothing. Soon as you'd come out she got that twitch in her legs, her muscles already thinking of running. I wanted to check her, I said *Even strong women need stitches* and the way she looked at me – I thought she'd hit me! Even though you were her first birth, even though the bed was soaked with blood.

Another page, the coarse sound of it. I say, again,

221

– Anna.

But my voice is quieter than before.

– She told me to send in 'another woman' to check her. 'Any other woman', that was what she said. 'Anyone but you' was what she meant. But then she'd always been unfair to me. Had nurtured a dislike of me because it suited her. But I did it, I went out and got a woman, and when the two of us came back she was standing with a fresh smock swishing at her ankles. *Still*, she wouldn't lie down. She kept walking around, lifting up one of you and then the other, took step after step dripping blood on the ground. Tabatha begged her, too, begged to check her, to make sure she was healing, and your mother said *I'm healing already, I can feel it. It's healing the way it's 'posed to.'*

Thrum of wings at my face, feathers scattering me with woodland grit.

– I never saw her so much as stumble. No mention of anything so much as a bruise. Not a hint of infection.

Once more I say Anna's name but this time I can't hear it for the noise the bird and its wings are making—

– Your mother with her white-blue eyes that chilled everything 'round them. Always a little bit of winter, following your mother.

A smoky smell. The kindling, too much in the stove – the woodsmoke overflowing.

– She knew you were sickly, you know. Only ever fed you from her bad breast. Her left breast. She said it trickled slow because she could only fall asleep on her left side. That was the breast she made you latch to.

The bird, its wing – no, Anna's hand on me. Lifting me up by my arm.

– She decided sick was all you'd ever be. All that mattered to her was that Anna grew up strong.

The bird.

Inside my head, its flight.

Looking out from behind my bad eye which is lost now, as though dipped in the smoke coming up out of the stove.

– You can see that for yourself, can't you? Soon as Anna was strong enough to take care of herself, your mother left you alone.

Outside Koan's house and the woods have a tender feel to them. How long have we been inside?

Anna's shoulder buzzing against mine.

Precious sister, next of kin, streambed partner, mirror twin.

Whatever she can see it must have a hold on her because she can't seem to look away – when I follow her eyes all I see is a plain old tree and yet her gaze is nailed there. I say her name but it gets lost somewhere in the quiet between us. She squeezes my hand which I only now realize she's holding. Looking straight on, straight on.

– It's all right, Adam. It's all right.

But there's a shake to the way she says it.

I don't want to tell her that my eye is gone, is lost entirely.

In the woods some small animal attacks another. The trees and their quick violence.

The feeling of being in that house after so long – realizing you swallowed something you shouldn't have.

– I shouldn't have made you see him ... I've gotten

numb to it. How strange he is. Maybe I didn't even realize myself 'til now, how strange he's become.

Phrases coming back to me, half and partial. Something about Mother. Something about Mother and her milk. I say

– We should go.

She nods because the moon is looming, but when we start walking she doesn't move as fast as I'd like her to, and it seems a long time I'm waiting for her on the stones. Soft bend in her neck. Night-time planet landing on our crowns, silver and cool.

– Come, Storm, we are waiting. We are waiting, Storm, come.

Before she goes out into the woods, her gaze dappling over me, I ask her if she's tired, and she says nothing. The gun is by the fire and she reaches for it, quickly, then pauses – looks down at her own body.

One time, she runs the back of her hand across her eyes.

So long as a wave keeps cresting, so long as it is always, always rising but never fully crested, never fully risen – so long as it is always climbing and you follow it skyward . . .

Can you can feel it, now?

I think you can.

I think you can feel the muscles tugging in your neck, your back.

Anna

Matthew came today . . .

Tonight Adam had to come upstairs to wake me. Sat on the edge of the bed with his hand flat on my low belly and I could see, as soon as my eyes were open, that his eye is a large black coal. Black all over. Gone.

What finished it? Matthew? Koan?

When we eat: bulbous and full, catching inside itself a shrunken version of the fire.

I'd thought, at the very worst, he'd say the usual things he says about Mother.

Your mother was a prize expert in cruelty. Cost her nothing to make a grown man cry. Said she didn't need a knife so long as her tongue was working.

The men would often say that – *'nough to make a grown man cry.*

Like that's so difficult.

It didn't work. Only made it worse. Waking up and Adam in the bed beside me.

– No, Adam, no.

His arms belted 'round my waist, the front of his

thighs wed to the backs of mine. At this angle, on this side of my body, it's his bad-sight eye that's closest to me. Little round organ engulfed with black pressing into my shoulder. I put a hand on his arm and deep inside myself I hear a cracking sound, the sound his arm would make while breaking.

– 'S early still, Adam.

Exactly how early I'm not sure but my tongue is wide and dry in my mouth so I can't have been more than a few hours sleeping. I think of what his insides must look like, to feel whatever it is he's feeling.

He is my brother.

He is my twin.

I try again.

– Is something wrong?

He's been lying on me long enough to make an ache in my back and my hip – my left hip, the hip that's taking both of our weight, is pulsing and stinging. Part of me doesn't want him to answer because if he speaks I'll know for sure, by the pull on my scalp, that my hair is in his mouth. And all it will be is another feeling he's made in me while I've been lying here sleeping.

But he says nothing, just starts moving in such a way while I lie here with my tired eyes open, picturing the small wet circle I'll make in the soil, outside.

Because that's all I can do, after. Go outside and spit.

If this were another day I'd make my prayer to Storm but now, instead of prayer, all the words stitched on my tongue are from that damn journal of Koan's.

Matthew came today, to tell me . . .

*

I think of myself in ten years, a woman asking me how I went on living, how she got here, and I don't know what to say, other than I thought better days were coming. Other than I thought nothing counted if I couldn't take care of my brother. I thought it didn't matter what living looked like so long as I had done exactly that – kept us living.

The day is so quiet that, behind the sheet-rustle sound, I can hear the waves breaking.

The wind must be coming from the east, in a straight line over the sea, to carry the sound of them that clearly.

Living for what, she says to me, this woman who is me, this woman I betrayed by letting her get older than I ever thought I'd be. *For what have you been living?*

Because it's early, only a few hours past dawn, there's much damp shade in the trees and it's the cool shadow I keep to, running fast and light because I'm running without the usual weight of my gun.

Running toward my hawk, who I've never seen in the daytime, never seen with the sun catching on her beak or making sparkle her wings' underside. I'm almost at the shore before I see her and in the dark of the treeline I fall to my knees – the sand already warming. It happens so quickly, night-time skin scorching.

But a few minutes is all it'll take to soothe me.

The look of her rising – her wings fluttering at their tips but other than that her body is a straight, swift line. The air pleating away from her, and though I can't see it I know it's there, her roving reflection in the sea. My breath cools me, now that it's slowing. Tempers the heat of the gathering day. The sand, even this far back, is starting to

228

singe me. My knees and shins and ankles, the tops of my aching feet. These moments of rest in the shade here with my hawk swooping, swooping and the sound of her cutting into the sky.

I know it's the speed of her flight and not the wind off the sea making the trees shift and rustle.

I know it's not the waves but the rush of her feathers that sets the cold surf fizzing.

Agile, winged thing.

Last true thing.

I don't need old crazed Koan to tell me what I do and don't know.

I know what the woods and the hawk have told me.

I know Storm is coming. Have felt Her move in my body.

But now: there is another hawk, and it flies straight toward her.

I feel it in my chest, their talons latching.

She falls backward, showing her stomach to the sky before shaking it loose, this other hawk, this maddened bird, but it comes toward her again smoother and faster and now she's moving her wings harder, pumping, but no use; together, they fall.

Were I close to them I know I'd see the other hawk's eyes are gleaming.

Inside its beak I know its tongue is smacking.

Has this been her daytime life? Falling over and over? Glistening hawk with her rich shine and the sweep of her wings I've known for so long as one straight, immovable limb made tumble, made waver, made fall.

Over and over they fall together and come apart and climb back into the air and my feet are stinging, burning, because I'm standing far out in the sunned sand, away from the shade.

At last, one final drop; deep and quick like a stone into water they've been swallowed into the trees.

My whole cold body burning. Not just in my chest but everywhere that I'm hard, in my bones and my teeth, the feel of their bodies locking.

And I can't help it. I know.

At the sight of them dropping, at the sight of her taken away.

I know it like you know you've been bitten.

I know it like you know night will follow day.

I know it like I knew Mother was gone.

Oh, Koan – what a trap you've laid.

Matthew came today, to tell me they were leaving.

Koan
Vol. 200
#99

Matthew came today, to tell me they were leaving. I often wonder what kind of man he'd be if he weren't tall. If he weren't strong. I wonder if he'd have gotten away with the things he's done. A man his whole life in the habit of dealing thoughtless wounds come, now, to tell me he's frightened of my behaviour, and that *I* cannot be trusted.

I laughed, when he used that weak little word. *Frightened*. He means to trick me, but he doesn't know how much of him I've seen, these years and the years before them. How dependent he is on Tabatha and what she tells him about himself, so that when he looks in the mirror it's not the sodden, rotten parts he has to see. He means to paint himself a very particular shade of manhood: strong without trying to be, open-hearted and forgiving.

I told him

– People turned to me. You can't know what that's like. Nor will he ever. He's a strong man but he's a sick man. And worse yet, he's uninspired.

Acting like he's forgotten *he* was the first one, to turn to me.

It shames him, now, that I was once his hot sun.

But I reminded him.

Reminded him, too, I'd have gone without rules but they asked for them. They needed the thinking done for them. The shock of it all was still thick on the ground and they couldn't look at a part without seeing the whole – they couldn't stand to see even a fraction. What was the point of it? All that terror? What kinder thing than to train them to love and wish for what would obliterate them?

– That's not the point. Why we came here doesn't matter.

Kept telling me he knows I know myself, why they're leaving. Said I'd felt better if I said it. Said we'd done the best we could with what we'd been given but it was time, now, to think about the world in another way.

– You have to accept it.

That's what he kept saying, like I was a child refusing to sit still at school. And then,

– We all have to accept it.

I said we don't get to decide what world we live in and he said

– Yes, exactly, that's why we're going away. Why we came here doesn't matter anymore.

– We came here because you couldn't stand to be alone. Dress it up however you like, but that's the reason. You were frightened and you knew if you'd people around you it'd be easier to tuck away the fear. You *leeched*, same as you've always done. All you do every day with Tabatha, same as you'll do when this baby is born – this baby you seem to think will save you.

He came toward me very quickly, and when he took my head in his hands – his wide warm palms, the thick muscles where they meet his wrists – I thought he meant to kiss me.

A laughable thought, but that's what came to me: that he meant to forge a kiss with our two mouths because he believed the contact would break a curse we shared between us. But he was pressing on my skull. A steady, even pressure on either side of my head. At first it was too strange to be unpleasant, this feeling. But quickly it turned to a sharp and panicked hurt. I thought of the glimpses I'd caught over the years: stories of his father, stories of his mother. A dead sister. His lonesome youth. His fingers pushing now on the pocket of flesh at the base of my skull and I could picture, already, the bruising that would come up around my eyes. Could hear only the blood rush in my eardrums. I stared him in the face and waited for some glimmer of regret, something which would give me a little solace, but he was more at ease than I'd ever seen him, his features marked with a kind of peace.

I thought *Now, at last: I've seen you.*

Smudge of fire still in the stove. Matthew still there, pacing.

Talking aloud: to me, to himself.

Had I been asleep? It felt like I'd blinked and night had come.

Matthew's eyes landing on the cage. His voice coming clearer now. It seemed for a few moments that he was talking to the bird, to my old sick crow.

– You want me to say it for you? Fine, I'll say it for you. We were wrong.

Taking steps toward the cage.

I turned my face to the fire, felt its warmth on my throat. Listened to him moving, breathing.

Doing something to the cage to set it squeaking.

233

– This bastard philosophy, this ruse we've been living.

And then he said what he came here to say. What's been stirring inside him. I let him say it. Let his voice wash down my back, thought *Let him take my bird to set her free and watch how quick it comes, her needless death, as soon as she's without me.*

Heard him moving behind me, carrying her outside, no doubt, holding her against his chest as he opened the front door.

– We thought it was the right thing, but now we know different.

Thought of the time of year, of the nights turning cold.

– We have to accept what we know.

Thought of the heat – escaping.

When he left I went to look at the empty cage but saw the crow was still there, old eyes on me. Her neck wasn't broken, so he must have smothered her. Looked at her wing that never healed straight and kept his hand over her head while he said

– It's not coming. Maybe it was never coming. But we know now – it won't come.

A high rising wave. All it wants is to toss your body, roll you around on its tongue.

But remember: water can feel like stone, once you've stepped inside it.

Anna

Koan on his knees.

Hands on his chest where he can feel his heart slipping.

Opening his mouth again and again but no words – not a single word, not a sliver of a rhyme or a lesson.

What does a wolf know? What does she learn from the taste of the cub she's eaten?

What does a tree know when it's falling? What's it saying in that last whining creak?

The upstream snake who knows you're coming, who started tasting you on the air the moment you got out of bed, what is it she knows with her body stilled in water?

These are the things I'll know when he's kneeling in front of me.

Things I could have known all along but I'll know them now, now, today I'll know and I'll stretch my whole body wide to make sure I can fit all of it: the look and the sound of a trembling Koan.

So radiant, so succulent I don't know how I didn't do it before.

Mother wolf.

Aching wood.

Serpent's oiled belly.

Koan turned to a lamb, shaking at the smell of his own open throat.

One last sound before the blood is gone, one last sound and all that comes – a bleating.

Koan, a lamb.

Bleating on his knees.

Koan
Vol.—
#—

sore head, lids peeled
too-open eyes
my dreams are syrup
dark, dark bird, her ruptured flight –
left me with an ache i cannot speak around
why so long?
why did you take so long, so long?

Adam

I wake in the night with my chest panging and I know it's because she's running through the woods and my heart is beating fast so that we don't fall out of time.

Then: I hear the trees crying.

Sound of an animal a trap has maimed.

Pulling a pillow over my head and letting the minutes pass but still: the high-pitched coo.

It has more of a flesh-sound, tonight.

More of an above-ground sound.

I get out of bed. I light the lamp and listen as its glow is growing, spreading while I look down at my pale knees, my cold feet.

The floor feels hot.

Burning, almost, and there's a smell, too.

Squinting in the pale light of the moon I see my feet are thickly lined with red.

I see I'm standing where Mother lay down, where she or something she held close to her bled.

I kneel and feel the red on my knees.

Feel the red on my palm. I hold it over my face and taste it, this lush red.

Tongue red.

Womb red.

– Mother.

Our mother.

Here, pulsing in the floor.

The wood so warm and damp I think I might sink down and sleep inside it.

The crying outside.

And behind the crying, the waves. Rolling.

A noise on the stairs: Anna come back too soon, smelling of smoke and fire.

But not too soon, because it's morning.

Looking at the red on my skin and on the floor.

She's wiping my face. She uses her dress, the coarse cloth grating.

Making me sit in the bath, lifting my legs in and cursing at the tap, twisting it 'til the water runs hard and cold. She leaves it running, goes away, comes back with salt, a lump of it I know she means to make me swallow.

She rubs her hands up and down, my arms and my chest and sex and legs. The red comes away easily from my left side, the side I slept on and kept warm and moist on the ground.

The stains on my right side turned dry and tough in the night and they hurt more, coming away.

I try to move away from the cold of the water but she holds me tight and rubs and rubs and soon all of me is numb and bright. All the soreness from a few days ago still fresh so there's not much new skin, beneath the red, to rub away.

She does my face last. Squinting hard at my lips, looking under my tongue.

How to tell her I didn't eat it? Didn't eat up Mother, only tasted her. Only felt her brush my mouth.

Anna says to stay in bed. Tells me to sleep even though I slept all night, says

– That was fever sleep, it doesn't count.

And so I lie down and watch her move about the end of the room, looking at the stain that's no longer pulsing but where else did all this blood come from? Anna kneeling beside it like she did when we first knew Mother was gone. Sniffing like Mother was a creature she could track.

But it was just a normal stain, then, already dehydrated and faded.

Now that it's come alive it might tell us something new. There must be a way to read it, to strain it – get at the words sunk inside.

Anna sniffs at its edges where it's cardinal, its centre where it's now maroon.

The tendons in her ankles thrumming.

She wets a towel in the bath and rubs at it. For a moment it looks still and dry, but then it fills up again. Slowly, from the inside out.

She says only

– I don't know.

And I say

– It's Mother,

I say

– Mother, Mother.

Mother standing in the grass, her long dress snagging.

Her calves a little swollen, the flesh a little bunched around her knees. But tall, still. Dark hair shining.

But her face is not quite right. Is not quite hers. Like her reflection in the stream: yet to settle. And she moves too slowly to be alive.

A stain spreads outwards from her groin, from beneath her mother-belly. Blood-bloom. The cream-coloured silk taking up the colour. But if it were real the blood would just fall down between her legs. And in the dream I'm certain I amn't yet born, that much I know – that I am that stain.

That slow spread.

That all night I'll carry on seeping, growing.

Maybe, after Anna had come, Mother forgot she was having another child.

Maybe she took Anna to her breast and only later felt me as a pang, as a slow veil wetting her thighs.

A little too long my lungs without air.

Little too long my eyes without light.

Or maybe she could tell there was something not right about me, and so she took me back inside.

I can hear the birds outside.

The ones that are black all over and the ones with the long white necks that for years we thought were called regrets.

It sounds better than their real name, Anna said. And so that's what we say whenever we see them. Look there, all those regrets on the horizon. Look at the regrets in that tree.

Alongside the birdsong: shuffling sound. A rubbing together of creaturely flanks. Sometimes, after Anna has killed certain things, their mates will come to the house and start to shuffle. Just far enough away that we can't see. The shuffling a kind of grief. The way some animals nurse a broken heart.

A shaking come over the ground, up through the walls of the house. The floorboards.

Can Anna feel it too?
She holds on to my arms to make me still.
Because it's me that's shaking.
My breath inside my lungs which are trembling.
I look up.
My own eyes, shaking.
An acre of skyline: rattling.

Anna

Mother's red come back. Soft impression on the bedroom floor. Nothing to do but kneel down beside it, sing to it. Nothing to do but pound the floor 'til my palms are cut, nothing but to drum the floor so that its juice refracts and shivers – if I can only make it jolt a little, splash a little, Mother will come, Mother, please, give us some sign – a knot from your hair, the salty water from your eyes – I'll take you in my own belly and I'll birth you on my knees if that's what it takes to find you here again I will swallow you slow and whole only come back, Mother. Come back and say it isn't so, a bliss that isn't coming, that was never coming – I'll cut out the thing I did the part of me that turned you cold: any limb at all, my face, my throat I'll slice for you, I'll live the rest of my life with your heart in my mouth and work to keep it warm only don't leave us here, torn. Don't leave us here, Mother – by now we must've hurt enough, lived in it long enough, there's nothing else we can learn from it, the heartache and the hurting come home, Mother, Mother, come home. Nothing to do but climb the trees I know hold nests and mouth the eggs I find there, move my tongue over their feather heat. One I could fit in my mouth whole and I felt the little animal inside, trembling through the shell, naked and moving. Nothing to do but put my whole fist into the soft soil and there, too, the roots and the minerals singing, my fist shot through with its quiver. Saying goodbye to the woods and what they allowed me to be, which is what I am. Just an animal. Some other animal and on my arms and legs I see it: sheen of feathers. All I am is an animal who lived her days between the sky and the ground, another animal dipping her shoulders in the water the water which looks black because the night is thick with cloud. The water turned a mouth that will swallow, uncomplaining, anything you can think to put inside it. Indiscriminate, salty and pure. The whales and their roaring flesh, a swarm with strands of lightning caught inside, a sister and her brother who have been waiting on red wind, red rain, red hurricane and I see it now, the red come through rushed with crimson rinsed carmine blushing ruby and puce rich with hum not wind and not rain and not the earth shaking only a woman singing since she was a girl only a boy still waiting to grow and the red on us, the red – I see it now, the wide red ocean leaving its red stain across the shore that's where we'll go, that's where we'll see Mother, Mother, I've heard you, I hear you – we're coming: the waves, that's where we will go.

Adam

Anna asks me to come with her into the woods and down to the sea.

When she speaks now it's with her new, lush tongue.

The things she says, and the shine on her mouth when she says them.

Words that are swollen, words that are ripe.

Beckoning, her hand warm on me.

We don't walk along the path but through the thorn-thick growth.

She tells me we need to make a more powerful worship, a more staunch devotion.

Pulling me over the last risen roots and holding me upright when it seems I'm close to tripping.

Walking ahead of me to stand in the surf. Up to her knees.

Milk sister. Mirror twin.

I walk out toward her and my shins are quick to start aching.

The sun colouring the sky a milky blue.

The waves come in and in and out and out – chilling us, the skin on her arms puckering, both of us alive with the cold.

'Nother hot sun, we'll have today.

The trees back on the shore standing guard and Anna's hawk come low, circling.

Might be it's circling us or something nearby we can't yet see – something wounded, limping.

The seawater hard and salted.

The rocks along the shore, we know they taste of it.

Her open palms on my neck and inside of my hands, like always, I feel her throat dancing. Her pulse is everywhere, her every inch of skin is filled with it.

She's talking but the words I hear don't match the shape of her mouth and my bad sight is moving. A thread, at first, but moving, thickening into my other eye, my good eye. Our hips press together and I feel them bruise, hers and mine. All this hard bone, needless wall between us.

– Hold on to me, hold on tight.

She's becoming different right in front of me, altered, new – Storm is coming, we've made Storm come.

I tell Anna

– You hold tight too.

Her blood running alongside mine, what her hands have held what her lips have tasted.

The sound of the waves and the hawk coming close enough that I can hear its wings cut the air.

The hum of the woods: watching. The black hungry for my vision.

The sea coursing 'round us and just as quick fizzing away.

Bubbles everywhere, littering Anna's hair.

Because she's in the water.

A strong wave comes but she doesn't turn her face away. She's facing out, out to the sea. Her face is washed over with foam and disappears into the hard blue shine and it's the shine I look at, the shine I watch fracture and slide.

– Just look at that shine, I say to her.

– Anna, that shine.

I look at it as best as I can with my eye being eaten – its sight disappearing.

The wave falls away and I see my sister gasping, the air a long tear in her throat.

There are feathers in the surf.

Anna's face and streaming eyes gone once more into the water.

The woods humming. The low song of the morning trees.

Oh, to have been another brother.

Another time, another brother.

Anna is limp like something left out in the rain.

– That was your mouth, I say to her,

– That was your sometime smile.

And the water all around us.

But never mind, pale sister.

Never mind, sister, gone from water.

My eyes sealed into buzzing black.

Sister, gone. Never mind.

A place I can follow you – into the water. We'll make a bed of the water.

Side by side, lying down together.

The gritty surf gone over head and my legs gone out from beneath me. Kind water; pure and salted.

A gasping sound, something passing through the morning air, a cutting sound. Low, swooping.

Is it Storm? Has Storm come?

No, it's only the hawk.

Still circling.

part iv

Caul

Eula

I always felt motherhood is a great sadness to deal a woman.

Even the women who take to it, the women who are happy inside their motherly skin. I think every person is born into a dose of sadness they have to swallow over time but that I swallowed mine all at once, birthing twins.

When you were born I thought that was the point of you. To make me live through my sadness all at once, and thereafter force me to be strong.

I don't know if you'll be mad at Tabatha for being the one to bring this news to you.

I know that you'll be mad at me.

I don't know what you remember of me leaving, or what you've forgotten of when I was still with you.

I don't know if I should tell you that when we first realized what was happening I could only think of the options that were unavailable to me because I was having you. I don't know if I should tell you that I wondered whether or not I should keep you. But you were so close to grown, and I'd gotten used to the feel of you inside me.

I'd have made a kind of peace with it, you see.

Eventually, I'd have made peace with it, if you hadn't been there.

*

I won't tell you things you already know, about how living where we lived could feel like the tail end of a scream that kept going. The pitch always just the same, always at the exact same frequency.

All I can tell you is what happened, which is that one night, I saw you, Anna, my daughter, kneeling in the stream.

I saw you tending to your body while you knelt in the water.

This young woman in the water, who was my daughter.

I tried to look away but too late: the shine off your hair and the creamy skin of your back.

Too late – my daughter's ripe flesh.

They say every mother thinks at least one of her children perfect but I'd never before noticed the slope of your collar and the pitch of your nose – how at ease you were in the dark. Unshaken by the fact of night-time. Unperturbed by shadow. When I was young I raced from streetlight to streetlight. And now, here, my daughter laying claim to a stretch of forest with the simple fact of her body.

I knew that I'd let loose my best part, and wanted to take you back inside me. I could feel it while I watched you. I could feel your body taking shape in mine. The weight of you, and your pulse. The size of you bruising me, heaving against my boundary line.

I watched my daughter in the water and I thought *Oh, that I could undo your birth. If your heart could live out all its beats beneath mine.*

No more than twenty feet away from me, and pointing your face up, up – opening your mouth to let the moon run down your throat.

Walking away as quietly as I could, knowing what

would happen if, just then, you were to see me and speak. The sound of your voice would ruin me.

Up the path, hours still before the first signs of the dawn would discolour the sky's inky hue.

I thought it was my bleed, come early. Only for the pain of it.

Not a pincering soreness, this pain, but an all-over ache. A bruise, but a bruise that was sweet. A bruise that hadn't formed to alert the body to any hurt or wound; a wound taking pleasure in the colours it dealt the skin. A bruise that meant to make me tremble as it was rising.

I put a hand over those parts of me that had been made tender, and I knew.

I felt it, on my palm. This new heat from that part of my body.

I knew it, I knew it.

I knew.

I made it back to the bedroom and then I was on the floor. Quickly as that, it came upon me and put me on my knees, that first wave, and the second wave put me on all fours.

Right there on the bedroom floor it came and it came and I bit down on my tongue because Adam was asleep in the bed and I didn't know what you'd do, Adam, if you woke up and saw me there, labouring.

The feel of it: a hot panic in every organ, like they'd all just that moment realized they were inside my body and that inside my body was a place they didn't want to be.

But also: something nectarous swilling inside me, looking for a way out and I was clenching everywhere I might come open because I wanted to keep the feeling in my body.

Suddenly knowing I was as much a woman as I was the stone inside a peach or the treacle-sap inside a tree.

The only way I can think to describe it: a fist that's been clenched its whole life, suddenly forced open.

A fist that didn't know until right then what it had been holding.

Making me rock to and fro, making bruises on my knees and palms that I'd only notice later, when I was leaving – I'd forgotten what it was like, such a simple bruising. Had spent so long staving off slithering, creaturely bites I'd forgotten with just a little weight and a little hardness; the things your own body can do to you.

I never thought I'd be a woman on the floor. This wood we all three of us walked over. I could feel our footsteps inside it, old thumps rising. There was so much we'd been told about red and at that moment I was still believing most of it. I can't say that it felt good, but it had the quality of addiction, and it leaned on the same parts of me that pleasure touches, the same soft pockets we all carry inside. It seemed that every feeling I could at that moment be having was rushing to that one part: right at the pit of my womb.

Liquid matter, so much substance I didn't know had been inside me to give, to part with it and feed into the thirsty wood. I wondered at the depth of it, thought the floor must be sodden, thought *It'll stain the kitchen ceiling, drip through.* I thought *Why have you surrendered, hard body of mine?* Another voice came through and though it didn't sound like him I knew it came from Koan: *You thought yourself so special, that you could live without a boundary line?*

When it was done and I could roll on to my back maybe an hour later, I saw it had all gone straight down, into the wood. Like the wood had all that time been waiting for it. And I was so tired, so confused, I thought I could fix it by cutting that section of floor away.

I knew I was leaving a strange mark behind. A mark that was maybe my shame at only half loving you, for being a shadow of a mother. But no. I know now it was my own deep fear at the way I love you, not that it was either too much or too little. I know now the love I have for you is the rough love of a dog that takes her pups in her mouth and the pups don't know if they're being carried or being mauled, if they're being brought somewhere to suckle or if their mother's hot, hostile maw is the last thing they'll know.

It was something I hadn't known about myself, that I had any question about the love I was giving you. Even though it was a love come straight out of my body and took enough out of me it might have been a third child. That was my ache, the substance of that thirsty stain: a deep and unseen shame at the kind of love I felt for you. Or at least: that's what I think, sometimes. The nights when I wake up and feel I've cracked it.

A feeling I hold on to until the moon is rising.

Lying on the floor, I thought of the two of you making devotion without me, and knew that I was being punished for all the times I'd dreamt of running away. I thought

Koan was right – being a mother had stoked the worst part of myself and my red came.

And to think of it, now, turns me cold. Knowing what I know.

To think of the needless torture I dealt myself by leaving.

That I left without kissing you.

That's how certain I was, that I could kill you with my mouth.

That after everything I'd kept you from, my own lips would be the thing to kill you.

It'll be no surprise that I dream of you and wake up with the red all over me.

I dream of the things I outright told you and the things I tried to tell you slow.

So long as a wave is rising it never has to keep its wet promise to the shore.

I don't know if you'll remember.

I thought if you could understand that image you could understand the truth of the small, drawn-out world we were living in.

When I wake up from these dreams and fall back asleep without washing the red away I'll dream of a patch of woodland I once came across where a mother wolf had just savaged her cub and in the dream it is both the smeared soil and our red bedroom floor.

I'll tell you what I know, now: though your lives won't be what I'd once, briefly, hoped and planned for you, no matter what else – you'll be living.

When I first saw the jellyfish, I thought *It's a trade.*
They're on land, and so I should go into the water. Let the salt
cut 'round my ankles and weigh my gut down. I thought of my
cured stomach, kidney and heart. Dried out and edible.

But then: the time of year. A sign that something had
readjusted. Something had come right, had fallen back in
line. Remembering what Koan had said – that we were all
slaves to the tide because there were things that only the
tide could tell us. I walked into them, to be certain it wasn't
some cruel figment. Made myself sick with their communal sting. It's not every creature that can hurt you like that
when it's so close to dying. Not everything has weaponry
stitched into its skin. That, too, I took as a sign. To be so
close to death and to carry on going, carry on stinging.

I know it will be hard for you to fathom, that it will
seem like a lot of time.

I know it'll trouble you, that people were hurt who
didn't need hurting. That there were people who, need-
lessly, lost children into the earth or spent their whole lives
alone.

I want you to know I'd have come sooner if there'd been
any other sign the planet would keep living, if I wasn't coming back to deal you a fresh bout of hurt right before things
were, in fact, over.

I never thought you'd be left alone, I never thought I'd
still be alive years later, coming back for you.

I don't think Koan was always the kind of man he is and
I have to think he did what he thought was needed. If I let
him be an unremarkable man gone astray then I can let
myself be your mother. That's probably the only thing I'm
fit, now, to teach you. How to absolve yourselves, a little, of

the things you thought were keeping you alive. Of the things you thought you had to do.

We're leaving at the same time but Tabatha will arrive ahead of me.

My red comes often and it makes me slow. No longer your fast mother. I've gotten used to people disappearing out of my eyeline.

I can only hope that when I do get there you'll have read this and maybe not have forgiven me but have started to think more kindly of me, and know there hasn't been a moment my whole body didn't ache for you. That I didn't most days find myself down on my knees praying to a god I knew was false, that I'd helped dream up, to take care of you. I hope you'll have started to know that I left because I thought I would hurt you, that the very fact of my body would hurt you, and that whenever the days first turned long or there was a first hint of snow I'd put my hands into the earth and feel you there, believing through wind and rain and the landscape shifting that even this was soil you, my children, were at one time standing on.

But if you can't know this, then know, only, that I leave tomorrow.

Know that I am coming, now, know that I am coming.

Acknowledgements

Thank you to my parents, Pat and Angie, for all the bookshop Sundays and all the other countless ways they helped me become a writer. I know how lucky I am to be your daughter.

To my sister, Ali, for the endless solidarity, the side-splitting laughter and for always knowing what to say.

To Dave, without whose sustaining conversation and constant wit I'd be very much lost in the world.

To Davy and Nelle, for their unwavering kindness and an enthusiasm I try to be worthy of.

To Rach, Aoifs, Grá and Lauren, for the wine, the unflinching loyalty and all the soft sits.

To Megan Mayhew Bergman, Deirdre McManer and Angie Cruz, for their patience and wisdom when I first put Anna and Adam to paper at Bennington College.

Thank you to the Arts Council; without the invaluable support of the Literature Bursary Award this novel would simply not have been possible.

Thank you to MacDowell for giving me a cabin in the woods, inside of which this book started feeling like the book I wanted it to be.

Thank you to Laura Gill, Mary-Margaret Kunze and Dan Sheehan, for their careful reading at the messy beginning, hazy middle and hopeful end of my work on this book.

Thank you to Jane Lawson and everyone at Doubleday, for the absolutely brilliant work they do.

As always, a thousand times thank you to Lucy Luck, who makes the most difficult things look effortless while making all things possible.

Thank you to Fiona Murphy, for her fortifying faith in my writing, her inexhaustible patience, and for being the most generous, considered and deftly skilled editor I could wish for.

To Conor, for helping me dream my characters into existence, for re-reading this book in its every iteration, for talking me down and for lifting me up – for being my person.

While writing this book, I gained and lost people very dear to me. My beautiful friend Aoife made a beautiful baby: little Leo whose dark eyes I'll always remember flashing in the Rotunda. And Nana, the first businesswoman I ever met and who taught me how to bake scones – we miss you.

Sue Rainsford is the author of *Follow Me to Ground*, which was longlisted for the Desmond Elliot Prize. She is the recipient of several awards and residencies, including a MacDowell Fellowship, and she received her MFA from Bennington College, Vermont. *Redder Days* is her second novel. She lives with her partner in Dublin.